Love Lessons
Talia J. McCoy

LOVE LESSONS

First edition. February 22, 2023.

Copyright © 2023 Talia J. McCoy.

ISBN: 979-8985364002

Written by Talia J. McCoy.

Lesson 1: Therapy

It's storming and I hate driving in the rain. I considered cancelling, but that would be a cop out. Therapy is non-negotiable, a commitment that I made to myself over a year ago. I realize that life is what I make it, and I want to make mine better. To do better. I realized a year ago that I couldn't go it alone. There was work to be done, wounds to be healed and I didn't know where to start. At a low moment thirteen months ago, by happenstance, a suicide prevention commercial caught my attention. I wasn't suicidal, but could relate to the examples used to illustrate when it's time to seek assistance. I felt hopeless. I felt stuck. I had a hard time defining purpose. I was so task focused that I wasn't living. I was just moving through life. Checking off boxes on lists I created. So I made an appointment. I was reluctant at first. I didn't understand the process. Was I to walk in and start talking? Would I be expected to word vomit my deep dark secrets to someone I'd just met? At what point do I admit my brokenness? How does this relationship work? I'm so glad I did it. So glad that I took the leap.

My attention is pulled away by the buzz of my cell phone. I look down to see a text from Maurice, "You look really nice this evening!" Out of habit, I look around to see where he is and spot him almost immediately. He is ironically seated across the aisle from us, two tables away and his particular seat placement puts him behind Mike with a clear shot at me. This is some stalker type shit.

At the abrupt sound of a blaring horn, my reflections are interrupted and I move slowly through the green light. I had slipped off in a recent memory and took a second too long taking the light. A right

1

turn on Sheffield Lane and half a mile later, I arrive at Dr. Drea's office. I don't remember the drive over. The drive was automatic. Like muscle memory. My mind is filled with stuff. I've made great strides with the assistance of Dr. Drea. I've excelled in my profession. I've been more intentional with my friends and family. I feel more fulfilled in many areas, except my love life. That is in shambles.

The rain and overcast sky make the day seem later than is, but it is 4 p.m., my standing appointment every other Friday. I walk in, hang my raincoat and take notice of the song playing in Dr. Drea's office. *"Experience is a good teacher. It takes someone like me to know."* I smile, "Miki Howard," I say to myself, making a mental note to add this song to my playlist.

"I'm making coffee, would you like some?" Dr. Drea calls from the next room.

"No thanks, just water please," I say, walking over to the window and listening to the jazzy song.

"The closed sign on my door, I had to tear it down. A new world of happiness turned me completely around."

The rain drops on the glass make the lights outside look like distorted painted dots. *The closed sign on my door.* These words cause a tinge of sadness that I don't exactly understand. For some strange reason I feel shame. I feel confused. Is there a closed sign on *my* door? At that very moment, Dr. Drea returns with a mug of coffee and a bottled water. She sits both of them on the glass tabletop, breaking my trance. I move to the sofa across from her. We lock eyes and with a half-smile I feel the warm wetness of tears streaming down my cheeks. We sit in silence. Dr. Drea is patient with me, her gaze reassuring.

"I don't know what this is about," I say, patting my face with the backs of my hands. There's more silence. She gives me a chance to find the words unsolicited. Her therapy style is like nothing I've ever experienced. Her warm and patient silence and reassuring look allow me the opportunity to gather my thoughts and find the words.

"I-I feel unsettled. I feel disorganized and confused," more tears fall, but I can't wipe them all so I give up. There is a box of Kleenex in an intricate golden cover with Amethyst stone detail. I focus in on the box but don't reach for a Kleenex and Dr. Drea doesn't offer one. She's silently granting me permission to cry even though I haven't fully grasped the reason for the tears. "I don't know what's wrong with me. I like this song. It's a good song, but for some reason, it hits differently today."

Dr. Drea turns the music off, "Tabitha, what about the song hits differently today?"

"I have a closed sign on my door, but I don't know how or if I can tear mine down. I know that, ultimately, I want the love that she sings about. A love under new management. I just don't know how to get there. It makes me think of all of the experiences that I've had. Love. What I thought was love. Lust. Infatuation. Romance. Sex. Flings. All of it ends the same."

"You got all of that from this song?"

"Well this stuff has *been* on my mind. Walking in here to that song, sent a rush of emotion. Like it's time to process and unpack some things. I thought about not coming today because of the rain, but I came anyway. Then I walk in to that song and for some reason it hit me hard that my love life is a complete mess and I don't know how to fix it. I know what I want ultimately, I think I do anyway. I just don't know how to get there. I find myself in similar situations with new people that ends in the same pain time and again. Just when I think I'm healed, I'm slapped in the face and brought back to reality."

"What do you mean?"

"I thought I've been doing great work and making progress here, but it seems that in some areas of my life, I have not. I don't see the same rate of growth."

"What areas, Tabitha?"

"My love life namely. I'm about to be 35 years old and I'm still doing the same shit I was doing in college. Hell, high school."

"And what's that?"

Taking a moment to find the words, I gaze back at the distorted painted dots on the window, "Superficial relationships for no other reason but to pass the time and to have companionship when I want it. I ignore it when I don't. Just doing shit, just to be doing shit."

"Do you want a more serious relationship?"

I return my attention to Dr. Drea. She has her hands wrapped around her coffee cup. I watch the steam rise avoiding her eyes. "I do, but I don't know if I am capable," I pause, searching for more words. I breathe in deep, "I feel like with all of the bullshit I've experienced with relationships, I honestly don't know how to do it. At my big age, I don't know how to be in a real relationship."

I look at Dr. Drea's face. She offers a comforting smile, "Tabitha where did you learn about relationships and love?"

I sit back on the loveseat. I relax more, "My parents seem to have a great love. A happy marriage. I'd say that's a good example."

"OK, but where did you learn how to be *in* a relationship? Your parents show you that it's possible, but what about the functionality of a relationship, the practical parts? How do you think a couple gets to have what your parents have?"

Whew I think. I hadn't ever considered the logistics of a relationship. "I honestly don't know, Dr. Drea. No one teaches that part. I never expected my parents to provide any details about the inner workings of their relationship. I see that as inappropriate. I suppose I only saw the intimate details of love, a romantic relationships from movies or TV shows. I feel like experience should teach us somethings too. Like Miki Howards says, experience is a good teacher."

"What has experience taught you, Tabitha? Surely you have some experience that weren't superficial."

The tears start again as I realize that a lot of my lessons were not positive. After a long pause filled with hurtful memories that rush my mind I say, "I learned a few things from each situation I suppose," I take a moment to quickly recall past moments, "I feel I paid a hefty price a lot of times," My voice quivers, "My self-esteem took a few hits. I turned inward. I feel broken and unworthy sometimes. A lot of the time. I would try to keep things superficial to avoid being hurt."

Another long pause and more of Dr. Drea's silence and patience passes. I take a deep breath and twirl my locs. "I've had some good experiences too. Those experiences keep me hopeful and trying. I'd also say that all lessons learned can be for my good. I just have to find the lesson in the pain, I guess," The distorted painted dots have my attention again. I continue as if speaking to myself or the painted dots, "I know I can't get what I want by doing the same crap."

"What do you ultimately want, Tabitha?"

"Ultimately? I want to get married one day. Have children," I return my gaze to Dr. Drea. This time making eye contact, confident in my answer.

"And immediately?" Dr. Drea's raised eyebrow makes me feel like she's thinking *check*.

"Mmmm," a good question. *My immediate actions aren't getting me any closer to my ultimate goal. I keep making the same damn mistakes over and over again. Can I even call them mistakes at this point?*

Dr. Drea breaks my internal ramblings, "Tabitha?"

"Oh. Sorry," I offer, realizing there is a question hanging in the air. "I want to experience real love. I want sincere intimacy and not just sex." I pause to gather my thoughts. "You know, I had to look up the definition of intimacy because I wondered if I had it wrong. I thought that maybe my idea of it was misplaced or outdated since it seemed so elusive. I learned that intimacy is defined as close familiarity or friendship: closeness. Yes, sex is a form of intimacy, physical intimacy, but it is not the total picture. I point this out because my misconception of this simple word has caused many a problem in my life," A deep breath before I admit to my naiveté, "In all honesty, Dr. Drea, I thought that I would have received intimacy by way of sex, which led to having sex with people I didn't necessarily care for or want for that matter, just to feel a closeness."

"What do you think now?"

I chuckle, "I think I gave a lot of good coochie to a lot of undeserving assholes in hopes of getting something they were incapable of giving."

I pause to let that sink in. This is new territory for me and Dr. Drea. We have talked about my family, my career, my friends, but never my love life. Running through my mental Rolodex of relationships and encounters makes my head hurt. The brokenness and confusion I felt coming in here today was magnified at the thought that I had come to a place in my life of my own doing. I realized in this instant that I had been looking for something that could not be found externally. There was something that needed mending on the inside of me.

"What are you thinking, Tabitha?"

My trance broken I reply, "I'm thinking about how jacked up I am. I have just now become aware that the hole I was trying to fill could not have been filled by external means."

Dr. Drea leans to her left, resting her elbow on the arm of her chair. Her hands clasped. Her full attention on me, "Go on."

Taking a moment to collect my thoughts, I study her. Dr. Drea is a petite lady, like me. I take note of her outfit and her hair. Her overall presentation. She is calm and confident. She is attentive. I think about myself. I briefly compare. I consider my choices. The successes. The stagnation in some areas that I have felt for some time. Where do I start?

"I'd say I lived a charmed life," I say, returning my attention to the session, "as an only child, my parents spoiled me. I had everything I wanted. The best toys and playthings. The best clothes. Hell, I was driving a Mercedes in the 11th grade. My parents weren't strict. I was permitted to do many things that other kids my age were not, but my social learning was very trial and error. I learned to navigate that on my own. I don't know what was missing exactly or how I would have preferred to get a social education, but I was searching for something."

Dr. Drea offers a comforting smile, "Are you still searching for that something?"

I pause, unsure, "I don't know."

"How will you know the search is over?"

"I don't know that either."

"So what's your goal here for this area of your life, Tabitha?"

My eyes start to fill again, "I just don't want to feel broken anymore. I don't want to feel as if love will always be out of reach for me. I want to feel real love. Real intimacy and not just sex. I'm tired of the indecisiveness."

"Do you feel your life was devoid of love?"

"No," I sniffle and reach for a Kleenex from the pretty jeweled box, "I know my family loves me. I know that my close friends love me. I just don't know what the genuine love of a significant other should be. I want to know what that feels like."

"If you don't know what it feels like, how do you know you haven't had it?"

"Mmmm. I suppose by the fact that I've been single and lonely most of my adult life. Still finding myself in immature situations with the opposite sex."

"Let's look at a different perspective. Say you had it, but because you couldn't recognize it for what it was, you allowed it to slip away."

Checkmate.

"Damn! That's a hell of a perspective," I say out loud. I think for a bit, my focus back on the intricate Kleenex box with the beautiful stones while I twirl the unused Kleenex between my fingers, "I'll consider that," I finally muster.

"Are you seeing anyone now?" Dr. Drea asks with a hopeful smile.

I laugh nervously because I hadn't planned to bring up my current situation. Shame keeps me from maintaining eye contact. I count the stones on the Kleenex box. I see seven from where I'm seated. "I'm exploring my options with two guys right now." I realize as soon as I say it that this situation is why I feel so unsettled. So confused. So broken.

As if to see the epiphany on my face, Dr. Drea asks, "What's that I see?" Her hand motions a circle around my face.

I look at her and draw my bottom lip in between my teeth in preparation for telling her that my love history is repeating itself. "I just realized that unless I can get to the root of the brokenness I feel, I will keep doing the same shit. I've got to fill these holes."

"This brokenness, tell me more about that."

"I feel that the past relationships I have experienced took something from me. Broke me in a way. My goal is to piece myself back together, fragment by fragment. The broken, scarred, and damaged pieces are parts of me. Maybe I should embrace them. I'd be a living, breathing Kintsugi. That is my hope."

"That sounds great, Tabitha. Where will you start with the mending?"

"I suppose I need to find the lessons. Uncover the holes. Maybe I can take a retrospective look at my history, own my role in things. As you've said many times before, I need to take accountability. So, looking at things from the alternate perspective that you provided, maybe it's always been me against me. So, I'm looking for the lessons." I feel optimistic, "I've always kept a journal, so going back through them will be interesting. I'll get to revisit my thoughts processes through time and examine things. Look for themes and habits."

Dr. Drea leans in towards me, "Where will you start? Your first kiss?"

"Maybe I should. It was definitely something I did because the boy wanted to. My sixth grade self would only say that kissing with tongue felt weird," we both laugh. It's so nice when we end the session on a lighter note.

When I leave Dr. Drea's, I find "Love Under New Management" on Amazon Music once I get in the car and listen to it on repeat the entire 30 minute drive home.

Lesson 2: Tabitha

I love the feeling of the sand between my toes. The warm sun beaming on my back. Watching the waves move in and out of the shoreline; it's pure paradise. I could sit out here all day soaking up the sweet perfection of God's creation. The beach and the water have always been so peaceful and comforting. Maybe it's the Pisces in me. Being near water is soothing. The peace and tranquility of being near water seems to heal me. I can hear the jazz playing from my bungalow, a little Miles Davis and John Coltrane aid me in slipping in and out of day dreams. Water and music are the best conduits to fantasy land. I decided to take this trip to paradise a week after my last session with Dr. Drea. The start of my journey. Coming back to a place that has been symbolic of new beginnings for as long as I can remember.

My parents brought me here for the first time when I was five. I don't remember the story, but my daddy says that he and my mom asked what I wanted for my fifth birthday and I simply replied, "the beach." Coming to the beach as a child was oftentimes the only break I would get. My parents kept me pretty busy: I was taught to work hard, to move towards excellence, and I sought the approval of my parents at every turn. I took ballet, piano lessons, and was on the swim team starting at age five. Tenacity was ingrained in me. In my mind, hard work brings my heart's desire. If my parents approved, I received great rewards. There was, however, a cost for working so hard to please my parents and to maintain such high status. I didn't have many friends outside of teammates and cousins. There were no sleepovers with classmates. The friends that I did make, were sometimes not the best influences. I wasn't taught about dating and boys, only told I didn't have time for that. My parents avoided the topic and kept me busy. They meant well, but never taught me how to be a friend, a girlfriend, or a woman for that matter. Trial and Error were my teachers. Karma my principal and Experience would become my advisor.

I'm an introvert by nature. A creative mind who prefers fantasies, daydreams, books, movies, and music. I love to tell stories, so I write. My journals are where I can not only tell the unadulterated truth about the goings on in my life, but I record poems, stories, and turn random thoughts into prose. To be able to share my experiences and make them sound as if they belong on the screen brings me great joy. Dance has also been a creative outlet for me. When my brain gets so bogged down that I can't write, music and dance are my go-to methods to remove the blocks. Any way for me to escape the pressures of my day to day is my jam. What's interesting is that I didn't always *act* like an introverted creative who favored solitude over being the center of attention. Once upon a time I had a very active social life with a plethora of experiences. I felt the most free doing things that I enjoyed, or the things that I decided fit me and my life instead of what my parents told me to do.

As I reminisce on the highs and lows, bumps and bruises, losses and successes I have experienced, I can't help but notice the changes in myself. I remember a time when I felt extremely confident. I felt like I could do whatever I set my mind to. In hindsight, I can recall that even with such confidence, underneath it was still a level of uncertainty and insecurity. It was as if there were two of me.

So how did that happen? Where did the lack of assuredness begin? I was unrecognizable at times and desperately wanted to change that. I need to discover the true Tabitha. I no longer want my representative to show up. I no longer want to reserve my true self for moments of guaranteed acceptance. There was no such thing.

Sophomore year in college is when I started realize who I really was. It was a struggle to admit that to myself. I was about 31 when I accepted that realization. Now here I am, at 35 trying to merge acceptance with action more consistently. I started going to therapy when I asked myself, *"How do I live day to day as who I understand myself to be? How do I go through life being unapologetically Tabitha?"* Those are hard questions to answer. It's almost as hard as coming the realization in the first place.

The simple idea of it is that I have to abandon the cares of other people's judgement. I have to remind myself regularly that I can no longer waste energy worrying about what someone may say about me because people are going talk regardless. This is a hard pill to swallow for me because I've lived the majority of my life trying to please other people. People pleasing has caused me to be indecisive about many things. I spent so much of my life stifling my voice.

In starting to uncover the mysteries of Tabitha, I unearth more questions. I examine all aspects of my life and ask myself, *Why do I do this? Why did I do that? Who taught me this? Why am I holding on to that?* I shine a light in the shadows, expose the lies and embrace the truths. So here in my paradise, my focus is on the lessons I can learn from past relationships and interactions so that I can examine the role *I* played.

One thing that I learned in therapy is that sometimes, the only way to get to the desired result is to sit in the mess. I need to explore patterns of my past in order to shape my future in the most informed way. Dr. Drea had provided some prompts for direction as I uncover things I have ignored. Some call it shadow work, some simply call it healing old wounds. No matter the phrase or term, it's about to get real. Dr. Drea had asked me where I would start, I suppose high school is as good a place as any. So here at my family's beach house, with old journals at my feet, I begin my work.

I look at my reflection in the water, waiting for the sun to set. Sunsets in paradise make everything better. They are the best part of coming here. Seeing the sky turn a mix of pink, orange, and blue with a tinge of purple makes me wish I had my camera to capture the beauty. The song switches to "In a Sentimental Mood" and I am immediately transported back to high school. Back when *Love Jones* became everyone's favorite movie and when finger snaps during poetry slams was the preferred method to show appreciation. Maybe this particular song is a sign that I need to get on with this retrospective study of love.

Lesson 3: Tim & DeAndre'

I was sixteen when I lost my virginity. It was quite an interesting and eventful day, but aside from the fact that I was no longer a virgin, it was nothing to brag about. See, one day before school, I gave up the goods to a guy that I didn't really know or even like. I felt the peer pressure of Keisha, a so called friend I met in Spanish class during the first week of tenth grade.

"You're still a virgin?" she laughed. I made the admission naively thinking that I wasn't uncommon in that. I didn't understand what was so damn funny. She must have noticed the perplexed look and the subsequent resting bitch face that overtook me as she composed herself, because she continued, "Most girls have lost their virginity before now, Tabitha. Ain't nothing wrong with you, it's just not the norm, ya know."

No I didn't know. I hadn't thought about what sex would be like before this conversation. I didn't think of boys in that way. I mean, I took notice of a cute guy, but that was about it. I began to wonder if other girls thought like Keisha. Was I delayed? Was I supposed to be thinking of boys and sex? My thoughts were interrupted, "Girl, you ok?"

"Yeah, I'm fine," I lied.

"Whachu thinking?"

"Nothing at all, Keisha," I lied again.

"Do you know Tim? The guy that drive that blue box Chevy."

"I don't think so."

"Yes you do. He bought your lunch the other day."

"Oh yeah, Tim." There wasn't much remarkable about him except that he paid for my nachos and had a car. I don't think I knew his name until Keisha said it.

"I think he like you," Keisha said, picking at her cuticle. "He gotta wait in line though 'cause I already told my cousin about you."

"What did you tell your cousin?"

"That I had a friend in school that's cute with a Halle Berry haircut. He like girls that get they hair done."

I was confused. I didn't know what she was getting at, but I was curious. "What's his name?"

"DeAndre. He go to Magnolia High and play football. A lot of girls like him at his school."

"Ok, and what did you tell him about me?"

"That I had a cute friend that I could hook him up with. He said, 'what she look like' and I showed him your picture and he said 'bet,' that's about it. His coach 'bout to move him to the starting lineup because he so good. All the cheerleaders want him, but he don't really be liking cheerleaders."

None of that mattered to me, but maybe it should. My mind was not on boys the way Keisha seemed to think of them. There must be a reason she was telling me all of this. I got up to go to my next class, "I'll see ya later, Keisha."

"Later!"

I went the rest of the day wondering what else I was behind on. I had an open mouth kiss the summer before seventh grade, but that was the extent of my physical contact with the opposite sex. I wondered if I were maturing properly. My parents didn't give me "The Talk" and I imagined they preferred to avoid it as long as possible. The remainder of the day zipped by. I didn't remember much of it because I was lost in my head. Instinctively, I walked out of the door of my last class as soon as the bell sounded. Still in my head, I didn't even stop at my locker and just headed for the bus line. I heard my name as I walked to my bus. I turned to see Tim and figured that Keisha must have said something to him. *Shit* I thought.

"Hey you," he said as he caught up to me. I kept walking. "I've been looking for you all day. Didn't see you at lunch. I was hoping to get you more nachos."

"Nah, I can't eat nachos too often, that meat on there don't always look too good. What's up?"

"Want a ride home?"

Damn that was forward, I thought. "No thank you, I'm good with the bus."

"Well can I have your number? Maybe we can ride together one day."

Disinterested and reluctantly, I agreed.

I gave Tim my number knowing that I didn't like him. I didn't want to feel left out anymore. And more than that, I wanted him to leave me alone.

Tim called me twice a day for a week. The calls lasted a cumulative twenty-six minutes. My lack of interest wouldn't allow me to stay on the phone with him for longer than two to three minutes at a time. At school, he insisted on walking me to class. If it were possible to accidentally end up in a relationship, I imagine this would be how it'd happen. He bought me nachos one day at lunch without me asking. He did tell them to hold the meat, so maybe he listened to what I said. I had to tell him that I had already eaten. This was all becoming more than I wanted to deal with, but for whatever reason, I couldn't tell Tim that, so I continued along.

One afternoon, Tim asked if he could take me to school the next day. In this week that he had been sweating me, he hadn't bothered again to offer me a ride from school, let alone *to* school. I agreed and told him that he could come pick me up tomorrow. On some level, I suppose I was hoping that he would forget. He didn't. He showed up at my house an hour before we needed to be at school.

"Why you so early," I asked, opening the door.

"I uh ... I don't want us to be late."

"It won't take an hour to get there," I said.

"Can I come in?"

I let him in and before I knew what was happening, I gave it up to Tim, a guy I didn't really like, before school one random Thursday, and it was terrible.

There was a little pain at the initial insertion and then a bunch of humping movements, grunting, and the occasional sweat droplet in my face. It was disgusting. Neither of us were completely naked. I didn't like him enough to really show my body. Maybe he was ashamed of his. If he wasn't, he probably should have been with his inverted nipples and hairy chest that resembled the meat on the nachos they serve in the cafeteria at school. It was bad and I didn't even know what bad sex was. I was ashamed and disappointed. I didn't want him to drive me to school afterwards. I didn't know how I would get to school or if I would get there in time to make first period, but I refused to show up with Tim.

At the completion of the longest two minutes of my life, I didn't even care much. I just wanted him to leave. There was nothing romantic about it. Nothing like in the movies. There wasn't any kissing, I avoided the opportunity. There was no caressing or gazing into each other's eyes, I didn't want to look at him. We only exposed the parts necessary to get the job done. I was so distracted with dodging sweat drops that I don't recall what the sex felt like. I declined a second offer to drive me to school.

"So you ok? I didn't hurt you, did I?"

I nearly gagged. I smiled and averted my eyes, "No you didn't."

"Did you cum?"

Did I what? I thought, *Cum?* I didn't even know what he was asking, "No," I answered.

"Oh well, I got you next time. Later." He finally left and I was relieved.

He actually thought we would do this again. Little did he know, I had absolutely no intention of ever speaking to him again. In fact, before I began to frantically figure out how I would get to school, I had already decided that I would go on about my life as if it never happened. And for all intents and purposes, I was still a virgin. For the rest of the day, my mantra was, *I AM A VIRGIN. Virgin.* If I said it enough, maybe it'll be so. Virgin! Now let me get my virgin ass to school.

I called my uncle, lied about missing the bus and asked him to take me to school. With no questions asked, he was there right away. I missed first period, but I got there just in time to make it to second period Spanish class. The very class I had with Keisha. No hello, no pleasantries, just a directive: "Ride the bus with me after school, DeAndre wanna meet you."

Keisha was up to no good. She knew that I was a "virgin" and it seemed she had a plan for me. I didn't want any parts of her ideas, especially after the morning I had. Sex was terrible and I was cool to never do it again. I went on about my day, trying not to think about the disappointment of this morning. I was so happy that I didn't have any classes with Tim.

I walked out of seventh period Science class and saw Keisha standing against the lockers. She was relentless about my joining her on the bus after school. Again, I didn't decline. As we walked to her bus, instead of me walking to my own, she tells me more about her cousin. I was dragging, not wanting to go and for some reason I wouldn't tell her that.

"He's dark with wavy hair. He plays basketball and football at his school and he thinks you're cute." The best part about what she said about her cousin was that he went to a different school. I couldn't fathom dodging two guys at the same place. It didn't dawn on me right away that she said that he thought I was cute. This must have been in the works since she first told me about DeAndre. She likely had been trying to get us to meet up since she discovered that I was untouched. She had showed him a picture I took at Sears Portrait Studio over the summer, right after I cut my hair. I then understood why she asked to borrow the picture.

The bus ride to her neighborhood was very different than the ride I took every day. Dilapidated houses lined the streets, junk cars rusted away in front yards, killing the grass. Keisha and I were definitely from different worlds, so why was I following her lead? The bus slowed to a stop.

"This is us," Keisha said as she got up and grabbed my hand to exit the bus.

I noticed a car parked out front of the house that Keisha was headed toward. Two guys leaned on the hood: one was just as she described, very good looking.

Keisha introduced us and the compliments began. DeAndre was very flirtatious. He licked his lips a lot. I suppose that was meant to be sexy. He asked me a lot of questions about myself. Some of which I didn't know how to answer.

The guys had a bag of snacks that they sat on the coffee table upon entering the quaint house. Keisha's house smelled funny. It was like a mix of moth balls and cooked food, but not freshly cooked food. The couch was covered in plastic and made a lot of noise when we sat down.

I was handed Doritos and a strawberry kiwi Snapple and DeAndre was back at it with the compliments. He touched my knee and I knew what would come later. I should have called my uncle, but was so consumed with thoughts of being judged if I left. I felt stuck. Obligated to follow through with a plan I was not involved with making. DeAndre stood, grabbed my hand and whispered, "Let's give them the room."

I hadn't even noticed Keisha and the other guy kissing as if DeAndre and I had already disappeared. We left the living room, allowing the couple to sloppily kiss in private. The sight turned my stomach. I remembered the first time I kissed a boy with tongue. It felt weird and I didn't know what to do. What Keisha and that other guy were doing didn't look pleasurable at all.

The only other available rooms contained beds, a toilet or an oven. I let him lead me to a bedroom and for the second time that day, I got into bed with a guy I barely knew. The best part about this encounter, compared to the first, was that DeAndre didn't look too bad naked and there was no sweat dripping down on my face. There was again a slight discomfort, a lot of humping, groaning, cussing, and a relieved collapse. I remember thinking that it was a good thing we went to different schools because I had no intentions of speaking with him again either.

So the sad reality is that on the day I lost my virginity, I had sex with two different guys. They were equally terrible and equally avoidable. The most interesting part of all of this is that, the story of how I became un-virginized did not bother me, I fully intended to continue on about my life as if none of it ever occurred. In my mind and by my portrayal of things, I was still a virgin, pure as snow. I had, however, arrived to the conclusion that I was lied to about sex. The movies were a big lie. My non-virgin friends were big liars. Sex was terrible no matter who you did it with. No matter how cute the guy was, it would be bad. And I was in no certain rush to do it again.

Looking back on all of this, the part that bothers me now is the fact that I felt an obligation to have sex to begin with. It was as if I couldn't say no. I felt that both times, I was past the point of no return. Where was my voice? Why didn't I go with my first thought and call my uncle to pick me up instead of having sex with DeAndre? Why did I allow people I barely knew make plans about my body without objection?

Sitting with those questions for a few days, I write my thoughts in my journal. I call to confirm my appointment with Dr. Drea so I can process this. I want to unpack this first encounter with sex and physical intimacy and discover how that impacts my current view of men and my perception of love.

Lesson 4: Calvin

At the ending of my high school days, I met Calvin. He was fine. Christopher Williams fine, if you like the fair skin, curly hair types. As for me, those qualities caught my attention. I never really had a type, I just like what I like. With Calvin, it was his style. His style screamed that he belonged on the East Coast. He listened to Wu Tang Clan and wore Timberland boots year round. He was humble, as if he didn't realize how fine or talented he actually was.

Calvin was a star athlete at his school, playing football and baseball, with ambitions to obtain a scholarship for one of the sports to fund his college education. The athletic scholarships would only be a means to get to college without his parents paying for it. His goal was to become a physician of sports medicine.

I met him through Keisha as well. She was dating his cousin and wanted us to double date. I should have said no considering how things went down the last time she wanted me to meet someone. We ended up meeting the guys at the county fair. Calvin seemed shy, almost standoffish. His voice was soft. He was chivalrous: asking if I was hungry or thirsty, if I wanted to ride the rides or play a game. We mainly just walked around the fair, people watching and getting to know each other.

Calvin spoke of his goals and aspirations. He was the youngest of five children and the only boy. I could tell that he was uncomfortable speaking about himself, but I kept asking questions and he kept answering. By 10 o'clock that night, I had forgotten that we were actually at the fair with Keisha and Calvin's cousin. We talked the entire time. We shared a funnel cake and tried a deep fried Oreo. He bought me kettle corn to take home with me. It was a good night. It was refreshing to hang out with a guy who seemed genuinely interested in getting to know me. He didn't talk of sex or make any inappropriate touches. Calvin seemed respectful. Probably came with the territory of living in the house with five women. They would be proud.

Calvin was different from guys I flirted with at school. His life resembled mine. He lived in a two parent household in an upper middle class neighborhood not too far from me. He had a large extended family who gathered frequently, just like mine. Our experiences and values seemed more aligned.

By the time I met Calvin, I had only had about three experiences with guys, my first kiss and the two sexual encounters; none of which were pleasant. There was the upperclassman who, the summer leading to my junior year, tried for three weeks to visit me at my home to "show me some things" to no avail. My experience with guys during high school was that they only wanted to have sex and they knew no more than me on how to make it enjoyable. Calvin was a virgin, a real virgin, not a Tabitha type virgin. He didn't ask about my sexual history and I didn't tell, especially since I had no intentions of doing it again. He assumed we were like persons in that regard and was content to leave the topic alone altogether.

After a few months, he actually asked me to be his girlfriend. Truth be told, I had never been a girlfriend before and didn't totally understand how to be a girlfriend. What was I supposed to do as a girlfriend? How was I supposed to act? I hadn't the slightest clue what any of that meant. No one ever taught me or spoke to me about what it meant to be someone's girlfriend. I mean, I had crushes and boys hit me in elementary school. My teachers told me that the hits and teasing meant that the boys liked me. I shared my lunch with a boy in middle school, but I don't think that is the same thing. And I had bad sex twice, but I knew that wasn't the same thing that Calvin wanted from me. I liked Calvin and wanted to do it right. I didn't ask though. I just went along with the flow of things, feeling my way through and winging it.

Calvin was good at being a boyfriend though. He seemed well taught and like he had good experiences. He told me that he had a girlfriend every year since third grade. I didn't have any experiences with being in a relationship. My experiences with boys weren't broad experiences. Calvin was different. He was affectionate, always wanting to hug or cuddle. Physical touch with him was pleasant because it was gentle and nonaggressive. He loved spending time with me and I enjoyed his company as well. We went shopping together, decorated Christmas trees, and attended each other's family gatherings. All with no sex involved.

After eight months together, I told him that I wasn't a virgin, mainly because I really liked him. I wanted to open up to him the way he had opened up to me. I told him that I had sex once and that I didn't enjoy my experience. Singular experience, I only told him about one guy. I felt my first bout of shame at an action I had taken. Calvin didn't ask a lot of questions. He mainly wanted to know why I didn't like it and if I would consider doing it again. I didn't have the answer to either of those questions at that time. Calvin was very curious about sex and made it known that he wanted to try it with me. He didn't press the issue and seemed content with just kissing and touching.

I learned to become the supportive girlfriend, attending football games in below freezing weather, not understanding a single thing about what was happening on that field. I was just concerned that number 32 stayed off the ground and exited the field without injury.

When the weather warmed up, the sport of the season was baseball. I didn't understand that much either, but when the family had baseball jerseys made with Calvin's number on it to wear to the games, I was included. I sat in the bleachers with my pompoms and personalized number 32 jersey, yelling for my man to score. His mother would pick me up from school for out of town games and ensured that I returned home at a decent hour. On those trips, dinner out with the family was a given.

Our parents became well acquainted and Calvin and I were trusted to be home alone together. We had made it to our senior year without sex. Our first time was when I was visiting his house. His dad was out back grilling and his sisters were out shopping with their mother. Calvin and I were in the house, upstairs alone. It started with kissing. Then touching. That was nothing unusual, that was typically what we did. He looked me in the eyes and asked,

"Can we?"

I still was not interested in sex and was perfectly content to leave it at the stage we had been.

"I understand if you don't want to, I just ... I just want to have this experience with you and only you," Calvin said.

"It's not that I don't want to, I just don't want sex to mess up what we have. What if you don't like it," I asked.

"Even if the first time isn't good, we can work on it together," Calvin explained.

I didn't feel pressured, but I did worry about what bad sex would do to our relationship. I took Calvin's shirt off, signaling that we could go further. I gave in. He took my shirt off and rubbed my breast through my bra. He kissed my neck and unfastened his jean shorts. I couldn't look at him. Nervousness had taken over. I don't remember feeling nervous the first times. I slid my shorts off and sat before him in my panties and bra. I could see his erection rise through his shorts. My heart pounded. My breathing shallow. He slipped his shorts off and exposed boxers that I had gotten him for Christmas.

He slid my panties to the side with two fingers and began to play with the wetness. I could hear the sounds and arousal began to grow in me. Still nervous, I was curious about sex with Calvin. I was feeling things I hadn't felt before. He pushed me back on the bed and climbed atop. The insertion was painful as if *this* were my first time. I tensed up at the discomfort. Calvin kissed my neck and began to push himself deeper inside of me. He pumped three or four times, let out a guttural moan and collapsed beside me. I stared at the ceiling.

It. Was. Terrible. I was convinced that sex wasn't for me. Like maybe my "coo" was broken. I still couldn't fathom how anyone found pleasure or enjoyment from it. Of course I didn't tell Calvin that I hated it. He seemed to think it was the greatest thing on the planet. Maybe it was a guy thing. It was like we were engaging in two totally separate acts. I'm certain my smile was an awkward one.

"I know that was quick, but next time it will be better."

Next time, I thought. I didn't know if there would be a "next time." I still didn't enjoy it, but I didn't have the desire or urge to avoid him. We redressed and went on about our day. The food that Calvin's dad grilled, while his only son was upstairs losing his virginity, was delicious. Calvin was more affectionate than usual during the family dinner and I just wanted to get home to shower.

We didn't speak about the encounter. There was no critique, no review. We continued with the kissing and touching like before. Every so often, Calvin would whisper in my ear that he wanted to do it again. I would just smile and nod. I spent two weeks reading *Cosmo, Essence* and other publications that contained articles about sex. I went into research mode on ways to make the act more pleasurable. I encouraged Calvin to read stuff too. About three weeks after our first sexual encounter, we found ourselves alone at my house. I don't remember where my parents were, but to Calvin, anytime alone meant time we could have sex.

"I watched some pornos," Calvin shared, sounding very excited.

"Pornos?"

"Yes. You told me to look up sex, so I asked my cousin where to find books about it and he gave me a couple of tapes." Calvin sounded almost excited about his new education, "I want to try some things."

I didn't know anything about porn outside of what I heard at school. All I knew was that I wasn't putting his penis in my mouth and he wasn't going to stick it in my ass.

Calvin grabbed my hand and pulled me to my bedroom. He flipped on the light and asked if he could undress me. I agreed. I sat at the foot of my bed and allowed Calvin to pull my shirt over my head. He lowered to his knees and kissed me. The kiss was more deliberate. He unhooked my bra and let it fall to my lap. He sucked on my breasts and I felt a pulsation between my legs. My body responded involuntarily to the sensation of Calvin lightly licking and sucking my breasts. I didn't know what I was supposed to be doing.

He stood and took off his clothes. He was completely naked. That was a first, seeing a guy completely naked and with a full erection. I had never seen a penis before. He pushed me back on the bed and grabbed at my shorts, pulling them off along with my panties. Now *I* was completely naked. Nervousness rose up again. Breathing shallow again. Pulsations between my legs.

He touched me, causing bumps to rise all over and more intense pulsating between my legs. He lowered again to his knees, pushing mine up. Calvin kissed my inner thigh. I jerked at the unexpected wet kiss. He slid two fingers inside of me, I looked down at him confused by how comfortable he seemed to be doing these things he saw in the porn videos. Our eyes met and he turned his hand and pushed his fingers in and out of me. I could hear the wet sounds. I jerked again and felt more pulsing. Calvin retrieved his fingers and tasted the wetness on his hands.

Oh Damn! I was shocked and intrigued at the same time. He then buried his face between my legs. He put his mouth on my wet vagina and that feeling was indescribable. I jerked and squirmed, but not to get away. I didn't want him to stop. The sounds coming from his mouth on my wet spot were loud. He stopped just as I was starting to enjoy the act.

He wiped his mouth and asked if I liked that. I couldn't speak. I didn't know what that was or what the feelings were that overtook me as a result. He stood up massaging his penis and climbed on the bed. He slid his hard penis into my soft and wet vagina and my mind was on nothing but the moment. What I felt in the moment, his hardness, his continued kisses on my neck, him caressing me. There were so many sensations.

I quit trying to figure out what the feelings were and just allowed myself to feel them. I moaned. He moaned. I grabbed his back. My toes and fingers started to tingle. It felt like pure energy was building inside of me. Calvin pushed in and out slowly while kissing and licking my neck. It felt like blood moved from my extremities to the center of my body. To the place Calvin had his mouth just a few moments ago. The release caused the top half of my body to involuntarily lift off the bed, I wrapped my arms and legs around Calvin, who at that time had his own release.

"What was that," I asked Calvin, shocked at sensations that were foreign, new, and pleasurable.

"I don't know, but it felt damn good."

"So you felt it too?"

"I felt something that wasn't there the first time."

We were both panting like we had run a mile. My comforter was wet and I felt weak. Then I got cold. Calvin wrapped his arms around me and we laid there for a couple of minutes before I realized that we were naked in my room with the bedroom door wide open. If my parents had come home, we would have no time to collect ourselves. We decided to wipe up, redress and go to Calvin's house for the rest of the afternoon.

It would be another three months before I realized what had happened. I enjoyed that encounter with Calvin and desperately wanted to know what had occurred. I had feelings that I couldn't explain. I had no one I could describe them to for an explanation.

I certainly didn't want to be teased about it. Before we named the experience, Calvin and I spent several months trying to do it again. We attempted to recreate that day and those specific circumstances, to no avail. Calvin finally spoke with his cousin, the one who gave him the tapes, about what we did. It was that cousin who told Calvin about orgasms and said that we both had likely had our firsts.

Calvin and I continued our relationship, spending time with each other's family and having sex occasionally. There were no more orgasms. The Valentine's Day of senior year of high school, Calvin gifted me a ring and asked me to marry him. Of course I said yes, because I had a problem with saying "no."

I was ashamed to wear the ring because deep down I knew that I was too young to marry. One orgasm, no matter how fabulous it was, was not enough to commit so early. We continued our relationship with Calvin introducing me to new people as his fiancé and me continuing to refer to him as my boyfriend.

He asked multiple times about why I never wore the ring. I never gave an answer.

During the Spring and while I was with Calvin, I started hanging out more with my friends who were freshmen in college and who I had met while working first my first job at a local boutique. I started attending college parties, sneaking in clubs, and going to Greek Shows. I became interested in sororities and fraternities and general college life. I began to spend more time with my friends, which meant less time with Calvin. I was also getting a lot of attention from college guys. I liked the attention, which further confirmed that I wasn't ready to get married.

Calvin took issue with the amount of time I was spending hanging out. He even asked me to quit my job, stating that he would share his allowance with me if it were a money issue. It wasn't a money issue. My parents provided for me just as well as his parents did for him. After all, I had been driving a luxury car for about a year now. My end of the car deal was that I had to put gas in it myself. The job afforded me with money to hang out and put premium gas in my car. What I was beginning to realize was that I wasn't ready for such a commitment and didn't know how to tell Calvin.

I was being tempted left and right with the attention of the college guys. I told the cute college guys that I had a boyfriend, attempting to not give in to temptation, but they didn't care. Then I got the bright idea to tell the college guys that I was a virgin. In my mind, I thought that would be a deterrent. Like, who would want an inexperienced chick, right? Wrong! This little white lie was like dousing a campfire with gasoline and watching the moths flock to it only to roast in the fire. Each guy I spoke that nonsense to, made it his personal mission to "pop my cherry."

The attention was wild. The temptation was crazy. So I decided to end things with Calvin. I finally told him that we were too young to marry and that we were heading in different directions with him planning to go out of state to college and my plan to stay in state. I actually broke my own heart with the breakup, because the college guys weren't Calvin and I knew I couldn't recreate what Calvin and I had.

Hanging out with my college friends from work, I partied like I was in college, often starting on Thursdays and going through Saturday. I became so disinterested in the social life of high school—my social world and activities had expanded. Half of the people I met during that time had no idea that I was still in high school.

I missed Calvin most days, but pride wouldn't let me call him. The days turned into weeks and then months and before long, too much time had passed to call. I wanted him to know that I did love him. My breaking up with him had nothing to do with love. I just didn't want to get married so young.

What I know now is that I also didn't want such a commitment after experiencing a college social life. I hope to get married one day, just not right out of high school. Also looking back on my lack of relationship knowledge and experience, I could have spoken up more. I could have asked questions. Calvin had older sisters who could have offered some insight. I befriended college girls who could have offered some insight. I sympathize for my younger self and her lack of voice.

Lesson 5: Shawn

Rebound relationships are not a good idea. I deeply missed the companionship I had with Calvin and rather than calling him back to tell him that I had completely lost my mind and desperately wanted him back, I rebounded. I began hanging out with Shawn, my piece of shit second boyfriend of about six months. It was six months' worth of time wasted, only to end up with hurt feelings and extra insecurities. I had known Shawn since middle school and always had a crush on him.

He was the total opposite of Calvin, darker skin, unathletic, and suffered from middle child syndrome, which meant that he acted out a lot. I don't remember many good things about this short lived situation. Shawn brought me a few firsts, though none of them good. This relationship was the first time that I was ever cheated on and the first time that I let my crazy show. It was the first time that I felt as if I wasn't good enough. This relationship was also when the first negative seeds were planted in my mind. I know it's crazy to consider that I allowed a piece of shit to have such an influence on my life and how I viewed myself and my worth.

I decided not to have sex with Shawn, he was no Calvin and I was still meeting new guys weekly. The lack of sex was no biggie for Shawn as I would later come to find out that Shawn was having his needs met elsewhere.

One Saturday after he went all day and night without calling me, answering my calls, or responding to my attempts to reach him, I decided to wait outside his mama's house for him to get home. Listening to "Hopeless" by Dionne Farris, I was fuming at the possibilities of what could be going on with Shawn. He pulled up after 10 p.m. and wasn't alone. I slowly walked to the driver's side of his S10 pick-up truck and in a low tone asked, "So where you been all day?"

In utter shock at my boldness, he replied, "I just been hanging out." His companion, situated comfortably in the passenger seat looked as shocked as he was.

"So your cell not working?"

"I-i-it is." The girl he was with was cute, but she had no business in the front seat of my man's truck.

"So why the fuck haven't I heard a word from you today?" I was getting angrier by the second. I opened his door and louder asked, "Who is she, and what y'all planning to do in your mama's house this time of night?"

He didn't answer and now the pretty girl in the passenger seat was looking down at her hands.

"Get out of the damn truck," I demanded. He complied. I took him by the hand, lead him to the back of the truck and lowered my voice, "*We* are taking her home."

"I'll take her home and I'll call you when I get back to the house."

"Fool, I'm not stupid. I said *we* are taking her home," I repeated and proceeded to walk to the passenger side of the truck. I opened the door, pretty girl jumped. The overhead light illuminating the mounds of make up on her face. It looked like she went to the MAC makeup counter in the mall and let them play in her face.

"Scoot," I said to her waving my hand, motioning for her to move over to the middle seat of the truck. Shawn returned to the driver's seat to drive her home. That was the longest, quietest ten mile ride of my life. I can only imagine what the young lady thought while riding on the hump of an S10 sandwiched between her date and his highly pissed off girlfriend.

There were no words on the way back to Shawn's house either. The two of us rode in silence while Ginuwine's "Pony" played on the radio.

When we arrived back at Shawn's mother's house, I contemplated staying, but thought it best that I leave. This situation was still highly tense. He pulled into the drive way and I hopped out before he could put the truck in park. I started towards my car, a 1993 Nissan Sentra.

"Where the hell you going," Shawn called out to me.

"Home!"

"Naw, you fucked up my night, you stay and make it right."

I took a deep breath and stopped dead in my tracks, only making it halfway down the driveway. Turning slowly, I had a little talk with myself, *Don't you act a fool at this boy's mama's house. He isn't worth it. Keep going and drive on home.*

I didn't listen. I stayed with Shawn. As foolish as that sounds, I stayed. I slowly walked back up the drive and followed him into the house. He led me to the den and apologized. He attempted to make the date sound innocent, but he failed miserably. Yet I stayed.

A month after graduation, Shawn went off to basic training with the military and followed by tech school. He wrote letters almost weekly, professing his love and appreciation for my patience with him. He said that he realized that he had "a good one" and would do everything in his power to heal any hurt he caused before he left. It all sounded so good, and to quote The Great Lauryn Hill, , *"it could all be so simple."*

I didn't know what the military was teaching Shawn or what they were feeding him, but the words in the letters he wrote seemed sincere. He was due to be home for Christmas and I was genuinely excited. I wanted to see if the words he wrote would translate to actions.

They did not. Shawn was supposed to be home December 18th. I called him on the cell phone he had before he left, no answer to my calls. I called his mother's house, no answer there either. I had become friends with one of Shawn's sisters and on December 27th, she told me that Shawn not only made it home as planned, but he was also was engaged. As in to be married. To someone else.

Heartbroken and confused, I surmised that he photocopied the letters he sent to me and sent them to someone else and ultimately chose her. I waited for him for thirteen weeks. I passed on guys who wanted to date me. I was laughed at and ridiculed for waiting, all for nothing. Shawn didn't even have the decency to tell me himself.

I moved on as best I could. I straightened my back, held my head high, and pretended that I was ok. The fact of the matter is that I didn't leave the relationship with Shawn unscathed; those negative seeds I mentioned earlier had been sown: one, men cheat when the woman they are with isn't giving him all that he wants; and two, when he marries someone else, that means that you aren't good enough. I made something that had nothing to do with me all about me. OUCH!

Lesson 6: Troy

I continued to go out to parties, now being a Freshman in college, I no longer had to lie about my age. I continued to meet new guys and have typical college experiences.

One such experience was Troy. I met him while having drinks with my girls, Chaz and Shavonne at a local bar. He was shorter than I liked, but very handsome. He had dimples, like me, and skillfully used the commonality to strike a conversation. He was witty. He made me laugh. And did I mention that he was very nice on the eyes? He bought me and my girls a round of drinks and when his friends arrived, they joined us too. We did not have to purchase a thing that evening.

Things flowed with Troy, it was organic and felt as if we had known each other for years rather than a few hours. We played pool and he ignited my competitive side. He and I shut the bar down, our friends long gone, it was obvious that our enjoyment of each other was mutual.

"So how long you been single?" I asked after taking a horrible shot at the eight ball to the side pocket. I had beat him twice and it looked as if my luck was running out.

"A year and a half strong. I hadn't felt like dating or meeting anyone new. The first time I agree to hang out with the fellas with the intention of meeting a nice lady, I see you."

"Are you flirting with me?"

"I am!"

I smiled, "I like it. I must tell you though, while I am enjoying your company and appreciate the niceties, I have a boyfriend who is honoring the country by serving in the Air Force. I am awaiting his return."

"That's sweet of you. I knew there was something special about you. I don't mean to sound cheesy, but the pull to you is almost magnetic," Troy said as he walked past me to take his next shot. His shoulder brushed up against me. "Excuse me," he said trying to get past me to position himself to take the shot. "Eight ball, corner pocket."

I couldn't stop smiling, "You know you aren't gonna make that, right," I teased. In all seriousness, it was a hell of a shot and if he made it, it would be a miracle.

"Wanna make a bet," he asked.

"I sure do. I'll take your money."

"I don't wanna bet money."

Oh Shit, I thought. My right eyebrow raised as if to question him for more detail.

"If I make it, you let me take you out. Just you and me."

"And when you don't make it?"

"I treat you to dinner." We both laugh at his proposal of a win-win for himself. For me too, for that matter, I was enjoying his company. "I am wondering, though if I can take you from him."

Troy leaned over the pool table with his arms outstretched, the pool stick strategically positioned in his hands. I watched as his focus seemed more concentrated. With a firm jab of the pool stick, the tip hit the cue ball causing it to bank on the side of the table. The bruised white ball rolled towards the eight ball, slowing it's motion on the way. The cue ball hit the eight ball slightly on the right side, causing the eight ball to roll in the direction of the corner pocket that Troy called. I held my breath and watch Troy rise to see if he was victorious. The ball went in. I was shocked. Troy seemed confidently relieved.

"I guess we're going out." He giggled.

The thought of someone wanting to know me badly enough to openly express his interest in me caused flutters in my stomach. I was beyond flattered. With butterflies in my belly each time he paid me a compliment, I didn't consider not continuing to get to know him. After all, he knew the situation.

I didn't see his insistent pursuit as disrespectful. At least Shawn wouldn't catch me coming home from a date with Troy. In my independent study of relationships and based upon the two I have had, I decided that spending time with another guy wasn't cheating. As long as there was no physical contact, it wouldn't be considered cheating. If I had learned nothing from previous experiences, it was that I could operate within a relationship without sex.

With our friends long gone, I had no choice but to allow Troy to drive me home. He was chivalrous which reminded me that I really enjoyed such actions. He opened the car door for me and didn't put the car in gear until I was securely buckled.

The song "You're Making Me High" by Toni Braxton was in mid play: "*I want to feel your heart and soul inside of me. Let's make a deal, you roll, I lick and we can go flying into ecstasy ...*" Troy bobbed his head and sang along. I laughed.

We drove to my apartment, singing to the songs that played during the drive. After Toni was Erykah Badu's "Next Lifetime," followed by Rome's "I Belong to You." My first night with Troy brought a sense of connectedness. There was obvious chemistry and requited enjoyment. It was refreshing. I could have sat in his car singing songs with him until the sun greeted us at dawn. When we pulled into my parking lot, I stayed in the car to finish rapping Lil Kim's verse in "All About the Benjamins."

"I really do want to see you again. I enjoyed you very much."

"I enjoyed you too and I think we can make that happen. Besides you have to take me out," I replied as I exited the car.

Troy and I continued to hang out with our group of friends. We were a fun bunch. There were bowling outings, more pool, and even a skating fiasco that ended with three of our friends in the ER. It was a fun time. I got to know his friends and Troy got to know mine.

We frequented one bar so often, we all knew the bartenders by name on any given night. I was even referred to as Troy's "lady" a time or two. I liked the thought of it, but it was a lie. Neither of us corrected the lady bartender and once the notion was made, we played our roles. Our bar nights became sort of ritualistic; about two or three Friday nights per month, me and my friends Chaz and Shavonne would drive thirty minutes to our favorite bar to meet up with Troy and a couple of his friends.

I learned a long time ago to limit myself with the drinks. I have a two drink maximum whenever I drink away from home. I never ventured too far away from three core drinks of either an Amaretto Sour with a splash of Sprite, a good Riesling, or peach sangria. I couldn't hang with the rest of the crew, their typical orders involved Long Island Ice Tea, Cîroc and cranberry, or tequila shots. Often times, there was no regard given to how anyone would get home. Sometimes they pretended the next day that they were too intoxicated to remember the things they did the night before, even though I was pretty sure they were in their right minds.

One night, the third bar night that month, exactly that happened. Troy was too intoxicated to drive home. His guys and my girls had plans to hook up before they even reached the bar, and my two drink maximum ensured that I could drive to my desired destination. Needless to say, Troy came home with me.

The entire twenty minute drive to my apartment, I wondered what this would mean to this good looking inebriated man in my passenger seat. Would he think this act of kindness, my being his designated driver, was a ticket to my bed? I believed that most guys would think it's a given.

Not Troy. We arrived at my apartment, he waited to be invited in rather than following me across the threshold. He asked, "May I have a seat?"

"Of course, make yourself comfortable."

He didn't seem too wasted, but better safe than sorry, "The bathroom is over here," I said pointing to the first left down the single hallway of my apartment. "I'll get you a blanket and a pillow."

Troy used the rest room while yelling through the door, "I appreciate your hospitality."

"You're welcome, Troy."

"Seriously," he continued while the water began in the sink, "You could have made one of my boys take me home and prayed we made it safely." He had exited the bathroom smiling. His eyes glassy looking. It was obvious that he was drunk. Troy walked up to me and continued, "You know you didn't have to get me drunk to get me back to your place. I would have come willingly sober."

I laughed, "Please believe, I have no intention of taking advantage of you, sir."

"I'd let you."

"I want you fully aware and participating at 100% if any of *that* were to go down."

"Any of what," Troy flirted.

If I hadn't watched him take four tequila shots and down two long islands, I would think he were sober. He managed his balance well and there was no slurred speech. "Any of what's on your mind"

"Tab, I'm just thinking about Waffle House. Damn we should have stopped at Waffle House."

"Waffle House on top of all that shit you drank? You're asking for ruin," I laughed. I left to make sure the door was locked and to turn off the lights Troy left on in the bathroom.

When I returned to the living room, Troy was passed out on the couch, fully dressed, looking as innocent as a drunk, full grown man could. I hated to wake him, but I wanted to be a good host, wanted him to be comfortable. I tapped him a couple of times, he opened one eye and said, "I'm good right here."

I laughed, "I'm not inviting you to my bed. You can get comfortable though." I pulled one of his loafers off. He agreed like a good drunkard and took off the other loafer.

Troy took off his shirt, exposing chiseled arms and a chiseled chest wrapped snuggly in a black wife beater. *Damn*, I thought. There was even a little drool. My mouth literally watered at the sight. I quickly retreated to my bathroom, took a hot shower and hurried to my bedroom where I lay with my bullet and the image of a drunk fine man with a chiseled body lying on my sofa. I didn't care if he heard the buzzing sounds and moans of pleasure coming from my room. In fact, I expected him to quietly tip toe to my room to join me. It had been a long while since I experienced pleasure at the hands of a man. But Troy slept comfortably on my sofa, not budging an inch.

I had toast and ginger ale waiting on Troy the next morning. I wanted to help ease any queasiness he may have after a night of drinking the way he did. He was very appreciative of my hospitality and commented that my boyfriend was a "lucky dude."

I didn't know how to respond. Troy was such a relief. A man who made it known that he was interested, yet not in a pushy or arrogant way. He was a gentleman, like honestly, who waits to be invited in to a place you arrived at together? I loved that about him. He was a breath of fresh air.

We chatted a while as I gathered Troy a set of towels and a toothbrush. He wanted to clean up, even if he had to put on the same clothes. He said that he could go "commando" long enough to make it to his car and then drive home.

The thought of him without underwear aroused me all over again. I wondered if I turned him on just as much as he did me. I slipped so easily into a daydream that I hadn't heard a word he was saying.

"What's on your mind," he asked.

I wanted to tell him the truth. That I had been thinking of taking him for a long ride, literally, in my bed. That I had been thinking of caressing his arms, tracing his triceps with my tongue. That I pleasured myself to three back to back orgasms last night at the thought of him.

"Oh, just thinking of all the things I need to do today," I lied, but I wanted to tell him the truth. I couldn't care less about appearances, about having a boyfriend hundreds of miles away who had a history of doing his own thing. I just wanted to tell my truth. I wanted to tell him that I found him highly attractive. That the "old friend" feeling was refreshing.

"So what do you have to do," Troy asked breaking my trance.

"One of my cousins had a tonsillectomy and has to be out of her apartment by tomorrow. I agreed to help move her out."

He responds with, "I'll help you," and heads to the bathroom to clean up. He says it as if it was no big deal. I was in awe yet again at how easy things were with him. What man who isn't getting any nookie, volunteers to help the owner of said nookie, pack up her *cousin's* apartment? Where do they make men like this and can I put one on hold? Can I put Troy on hold, standby if you will, just until I figure out where he and I can go, where things are going with me?

Later that day, Troy called asking where to meet me; he had a couple of friends who could also help pack up my cousin's apartment. We met at the apartment thirty minutes after that call. Troy was teasing me, I was sure of it. Maybe he read my mind earlier and learned about all of the nasty things I wanted to do to him. Why else did he show up at my cousin's apartment in gray sweatpants?

Don't look ... don't look, he will see you, I thought over and over. I didn't listen and I looked. *Damn, I shouldn't have looked*, I thought. This man was pure perfection and in that moment I felt the need to put him on standby.

He greeted me with a long hug as if we hadn't spent the night under the same roof. As if I hadn't nursed his hangover this morning. I struggled with myself, feeling myself ease my pelvis closer to his with the goal of brushing up against his penis. After all, those gray sweatpants revealed exactly where it was. Men know what they are doing when they wear them. I pulled away, I needed to have some tact. It was like the little angel and devil on my shoulders were in a battle against carnal desire and what was right. Good prevailed ... this time.

One of my friends showed up to help with the packing and I felt a tinge of relief and regret simultaneously. Shavonne walked up and immediately took notice of the gray sweatpants, I know this because I heard her say *damn* as she approached. Troy had to know what he was doing with his attire, but he looked so innocent.

We got the packing done in under an hour thanks to the amount of help we had. Music played as we worked. There were no breaks. Not a lot of talking. It was a quick in and out.

We met my uncle at a storage facility and the guys got to the business of unloading. Shavonne and I watched intently. All that was missing was popcorn.

Fast forward to December, I shared with Troy a few details of the tough time I was having with my relationship and he backed off a bit, saying he wanted to be respectful, but also let me know that he was available if I needed him.

I took a break from happy hour with the crew. I stopped going to the parties and social gatherings on campus. I was horrible with returning calls and responding to messages. I wondered if that was what major depression felt like.

One day, Shavonne gave me the most wonderful pep talk that included a few threats to harm others, but more importantly, encouragement.

Her exact words were: "Call Troy and see what's up with him. Y'all definitely had a connection and you were up front with him, maybe he was standing by as you hoped. It's only been a few weeks."

I smiled at her and asked, "Will you go to the New Year's Eve Party with me?"

The party was an annual event hosted by Troy's fraternity and he was sure to be there. Shavonne agreed. We got all fancy and dolled up and agreed to meet Chaz there.

Coincidentally, Troy was at the door taking money and tickets. I was relieved to see his big dimpled smile and all but melted in his arms when he hugged me ever so tightly. He whispered in my ear, "I'm sorry to hear about the breakup. I know what you were trying to do and I hate that you were hurt in the process."

I wanted to tell him that I should have made my desires known. I wanted to tell Troy that I wanted him all along. That we should be in love right now.

I didn't. I simply said, "Thank you."

Me and my girls entered the party at exactly 11:45pm. I had no New Year's resolutions, I didn't resolve to be better or do better, I just wanted that crappy year over with.

Troy entered the room with two glasses of champagne and offered me one. Drink number one for me. I didn't really like the taste of champagne, but I enjoyed the tickle of the bubbles. We began to count down, Troy still at my side.

I felt the urge to take the midnight moment to kiss him. We had never kissed before.

"10. 9. 8. 7. 6. 5. 4. 3. 2. 1 ... Happy New Year!" everyone shouted.

I looked at Troy, who was already looking at me. We gave each other simple smiles, dimples visible.

He leaned in and kissed me. In that moment, no one else was there. I had waited months for that kiss and it was more than I imagined.

It started light and slow. A peck and a pull back so that Troy could check my reaction. His hands cupped my face. I smiled and closed my eyes, signaling for him to continue. He did. Another peck.

I parted my lips as if to invite his tongue in. He obliged. Our tongues danced to the sound of the band playing "Auld Lang Syne." I wrapped my arms around his neck.

I allowed the sweet kisses to float the memory of Troy's chiseled body sleeping on my sofa. I remembered the very nice penis print showing through his gray sweatpants. My heart fluttered at the thought of us laughing and whispering in each other's ears at Happy Hour. Several months of interactions had led to this moment. I was in disbelief, thinking, *I'm actually kissing Troy,* for what seemed like the entire 55 seconds of that traditional New Year's song.

At the conclusion of the most passionate kiss I had experienced in a while, Troy looked me square in the eyes and said, "You know if we ever had children, there's a high probability that they would have dimples."

I chuckled and that broke the slight awkwardness that loomed as we both realized that we had the longest New Year's kiss and people had started to stare. It was a perfect night and I was so happy I went.

Two days later, Troy showed up at my door unannounced. I was slightly appalled because I've never particularly liked pop-up visits.

"I'm so sorry to show up like this," He apologized, "I tried calling, but when you never answered, I became worried."

My irritation dissipated and things made so much more sense regarding why my phone had been so dry for the last couple of days.

I invited him in and offered him a refreshment of the charcuterie board I had made that morning.

"I've been thinking the last couple of days about how we brought in the new year. I hoped that I didn't mess anything up between us with the kiss, but it was something I had been wanting to do for a long while," Troy said, "I must admit that I feel guilty and selfish. I had no right to kiss you that way."

I was confused, but he continued.

"I spent much of our time together content in waiting for you to realize that I was the man for you. That I was the man you should be with. So many times I wanted to tell you that you shouldn't have been waiting on any man."

Complete and utter shock. I was afraid to speak because I didn't want to interrupt his flow. My stomach filled with butterfly flutters again.

"There were so many times that I wanted to ask you to forget about dude. I wanted to move our relationship out of the friend zone." Troy played with his hands and averted his eyes. I was starting to worry now about where he was going with his admissions. "After a while, I got tired of my boys giving me grief, so I let it go." He looked back at me quickly with a sly smile, no dimple, then back at his hands. "So after letting go, I met another woman and now I have a girlfriend."

Slap to the face.

My mouth fell open, but no lusting drool this time. This time, the liquid flowed from my eyes. "Did you have this girlfriend two days ago?" I asked.

Troy dropped his head and said, "Yes," his voice cracking.

More liquid from my eyes and down my cheeks. I simply asked, "Why, Troy?" I didn't break my gaze from his face. I wanted him to see the hurt and confusion when he glanced up at me.

Troy knew what I was asking and said, "When I saw you walk into the..uh ... t-to the party, I knew I wanted to experience your kiss at least once. I needed that before fully moving on."

"Why were you at the party alone if you have a girlfriend?" I had so many questions. This behavior was so unlike the man I thought I knew.

"She was out of town. I'm so sorry, Tabitha!" He apologized a million times more. "I didn't mean any disrespect or to cause any pain. I realize that it was a selfish move and for that, I need you to forgive me." Now his cheeks were wet.

There was ringing in my ears. My blood pressure had risen. "I'm not mad at you Troy. I am disappointed, but I know that it will subside. I appreciate your honesty and wish you luck in your relationship."

I wanted to dismiss this encounter. It was more than I wanted to deal with at that time and certainly not how I wanted to begin a new year.

We stood from the couch. The ringing in my ears louder. *I pray I don't pass out on this man*, I thought. I was overwhelmed with emotion. I walked Troy to the door. It was a slow stroll. Almost like a funeral procession.

I admitted, "I'm gonna miss you like hell."

"You say that like I've died," he said, trying to make light of the situation.

All I could muster was a sad smile. We hugged. He kissed me on the forehead, both my cheeks and grabbed my face with both of his hands. I looked up at him. Our eyes welled with tears. He kissed me one last time as tears flowed quietly down our faces.

A few years later I learned that Troy married that woman. I was a ball of confusion, feelings of happiness, sadness and anger all at once. He was happy. I felt sorrow that it wasn't me. This situation is yet another example of my lack of voice and the habit of going with the flow of things rather than deciding for myself.

Lesson 7: Byron

One day after classes, I made a quick stop at the mall. I wanted to do a little window shopping for ideas for a weekend of hanging out with my girls. While walking through, a dress in a department store caught my eye. After entering the store to examine the dress more closely, I locked eyes with one of the workers. He immediately walked over to me.

His name tag read *Byron* and he looked a few years older than me, very mature. He was handsome, a Gerald Levert, teddy bear type of situation. This may have been the first moment I developed an attraction to a man with a beard.

"May I help you?" he asked.

"No, sir. I'm good, thanks," I said trying not to lock eyes with him again. His eyes were sincere, set deep and surrounded by eye lashes that women would pay good money for.

"Well, I think that dress would look nice on you. Let me know if you'd like to try it on."

"Ok, thanks." I continued to browse the racks while also checking in on Byron. He was checking in on me as well. We locked eyes several times. Byron walked back over to me after about 15 minutes.

"You doing ok?"

"I'm fine."

"Yes, I can see that," Byron said as he checked me out. I watched as his eyes surveyed me from my feet, slowly, all the way to my face. He lingered on my eyes. "You are absolutely beautiful. I'm sure you hear that often."

I tried hard not to blush at his admiration. "Thank you, I don't hear it nearly enough," I said as I continued to browse the racks. I walked over to the next rack showcasing a *65% Off* sign. Byron followed me. I enjoyed the flirtatious banter and tried to encourage it.

"So your man doesn't tell you that enough," he assumed. My encouragement worked.

"Nope! No boyfriend. I like what you did there though," I giggled and allowed our eyes to connect again. The flirty back and forth felt like sport. I wasn't in a state to begin a relationship, but a little catch and release couldn't hurt.

"I try to be creative. So tell me about you." Byron requested.

I could not stand this particular open-ended request. I never knew what to say. I didn't want to sound pretentious or evasive. I didn't understand why guys just didn't ask what they wanted to know.

"Why don't you tell me what you're trying to learn first," I played.

Byron said, "Mmmm, well ... I guess I'd like to know how I could *learn* what it would take to get you to go out with me."

"*Maybe* you could just ask," I tease.

"Ok, ok. What's your name beautiful?"

"I'm Tabitha."

"Tabitha, can I take you to dinner? I'd like to get to know more about you. I think you're gorgeous and want some of your free time. How's that?" Byron teased back.

So this is a first. I had never been asked on a date before and for it to be done so properly, I was intrigued, "Yes. I will go out with you Byron. Only because you asked so excellently." We both laughed.

"Well how about tonight? I get off at nine."

Wow, so soon. I definitely liked what I saw physically. He had a boyish smile that made me wonder if he was as innocent as he looked. At the same time, Byron looked like a full grown man. That made me nervous, but I agreed to meet him, "I can meet you back here by 9:30 if that's cool."

"That's perfect. It's a date!"

I walked around Byron's store a little while longer, not making a single purchase. Maybe on some level I didn't want to leave his space. Just before exiting the store by way of an upstairs entryway, a mannequin donning an all-black outfit caught my eye. The black leather pants were daring. The asymmetrical top was sexy. I had to have it. I had no idea where I'd wear it to, but I bought the entire outfit anyway.

Instead of going home, I waited in the parking lot of the mall until Byron was off work. It dawned on me that Byron and I had not exchanged phone numbers—how would we reconnect? I watched the employee entrance of the department store intently, waiting for Byron to emerge. He came out at exactly 9:30pm. I watched him look around a few times, look at his watch and throw his hand up in the air.

I surmise that was the moment he had the realization I had a few minutes ago, we had no way to reach each other. Good thing I was good at stalking. I flashed my headlights to catch his attention. He looked up immediately and walked in my direction. *Could he have known the flash was for him? That it was me?* I got out of my car to greet him.

"Hey handsome," I flirt. He looked surprised.

"Hey, don't start flirting with me. I'll like it and think it means you like me."

"Maybe I do like you ... so far."

He laughed and pointed across the interstate, "Let go to Chili's. It's low key and bustling with people minding their own business. It won't feel as much like a date as it will like old friends grabbing a bite after work."

He had thought this through, "Ok," I agreed. "I'll follow you."

Byron walked to his car, looking back at me twice as if to check to see if I were still there and willing. He drove to where I was parked and I followed him to Chili's.

We were seated quickly, without a wait. We were led to a booth near the bathroom. Not many people were seated in this section.

We should be able to talk better over here without so much noise, I thought.

"Your waiter will be with you shortly. May I grab you a couple of drinks while you wait?"

"I'll have water and the rum punch," said Byron.

"I'll have water as well and a strawberry margarita," I ordered.

I didn't finish the margarita. I'm not a big fan of tequila, but the choices of fruity, frozen drinks were slim.

Byron was extremely easy to talk to. We chatted about everything from high school to family. We shared fajitas and talked about all sorts of things. I learned in that one date that Byron had one daughter and had just ended a three year relationship with her mother. He moved back in with his parents after the break up, thinking that he'd be there a few months and had been there for a year. He said that it was because his mother enjoyed having him there. I imagine only a part of that is true. Byron paid for dinner and walked me to my car. We both agreed that it was refreshing to speak to a genuine soul.

"Thanks for hanging with me, Tabitha. What are the chances that we could do this again?"

"So you want to see me again?"

"I most certainly do. The way I'm feeling right now, I want to see you as often as I can. If I can't see you, I want to be talking to you. So this would be a great time to give me your number."

I giggled. Byron was not shy with the compliments and expressing his desires. I jotted my number down on a Wendy's napkin that was in my cupholder.

I asked, "Are you the kind of guy that waits a few days before calling?"

Byron smiled his boyish smile, licked his lips and said, "No ma'am. I'm the kind of *man* who calls when you cross my mind. The kind of man who lets his intentions be known. The kind of man who has no problems letting you know when I want to see you and *then* will do everything in my power to make it happen. You think you'd be cool with a man like that?"

Damn. I didn't know how else to respond, "Yes sir." With tequila inspired confidence I continued, "I'll always be cool with a take charge kind of *man*. I've never had one of those before."

Byron smiled a half smile, "Well I've got you beautiful. Buckle up for the ride, I don't typically drive slow."

I had no idea what that meant, but I loved the banter, "Well, I'm looking forward to it!"

Byron opened my door, told me to be careful and that he'd talk to me tomorrow. He was so sure of himself. I wondered how one came to have a genuine confidence and not a pretend confidence. I felt that so many times, this night included, I couldn't be my authentic self.

I found myself stopping at the department store as often as I could with absolutely no intention of making a purchase. I just wanted to talk with Byron. To be in his presence. If I stopped by and he wasn't there, I felt an immense disappointment.

Whenever we talked, we talked about all sorts of things. School, work, goals, backgrounds, family, exes. You name it, we discussed it. I had developed an infatuation for Byron. I enjoyed his presence in my life.

He was a good friend. He didn't press the issue of being more than friends. I believe he enjoyed my company and talks as much as I did. I valued the friendship we were building. I needed the friendship we were building.

With my attending college and his own endeavors, after a few short months, things with Byron tapered off a bit. A bit turned into months and eventually a year. Periodically, I would go to the store and see him. We'd chat for a good while and things cooled off again. He would call out of the blue. We'd update each other and things would taper off again. After about a year and a half, we ran into each other at a gas station. We chatted and caught up as if no time had passed. We had become pros at that. We were most definitely at different points in our lives. I was a junior in college, working, considering joining a sorority and enjoying life. My partying had slowed considerably, but I still enjoyed the occasional outing.

Byron had gotten married just two months prior to our gas station rendezvous. I was blown away. He never really struck me as the marrying type. I saw him as a ladies man, remember a Gerald Levert look-alike. Women loved Gerald Levert. Women threw their panties at Gerald as he sang "Answering Service" and "Baby Hold on to Me". I adjusted my posture. I wasn't as comfortable. I was disappointed.

"You look good, Tab. Damn good," his compliment interrupted my thoughts of Gerald Levert, love songs, and panties.

"Thank you B. You look good too."

You bastard, how dare you get married without consulting me, I thought. I was more frustrated than I had the right to be. We were friends no matter how much we flirted with each other. Neither of us made a move, or a declaration of a more intense interest in each other, but I was seriously angry that he was married.

"Hey, I've got to go, but I would *love* to see you again. To catch up and see what's been happening with you since I last saw you," Byron said. Still very assured.

"Yes, just let me know. My number is still the same ... that is if you still have it."

"Oh I most definitely have it. You're one of my favorite people."

Then why the fuck did you get married without telling me! I wanted to scream, but instead I agreed.

Byron called me a few hours later, "Can you meet me?"

"Where?" I was still perturbed and hadn't quite figured out why I was having such an emotional reaction to a guy I was only friends with marrying someone else. On some level, I knew that nothing was owed to me. At the same time, I felt our connections meant more.

We met up in a parking lot near a local bar, sat outside, and talked for hours. I insisted on a public place to maintain some sort of boundary with my now married, good looking friend. It was so easy to talk with him, it always had been. I missed it dearly. He told me about his wife, how they met and where they honeymooned. He seemed to love hearing about my college experiences. An old spark was reignited that night. As much as I tried to extinguish it throughout that evening, Byron made it difficult with his compliments.

"You have always been so beautiful to me. I can't believe no one has snatched you up."

"Well B, I'd have to be open to being 'snatched up.' Besides my crush up and got married on me," I admitted before I had thought that idea through. I couldn't take it back if I wanted to. And I didn't. I needed him to know that I was bothered by his new relationship status even if I hadn't completely understood why myself.

"Your crush?" He sounded genuinely surprised. "What you mean, Tab?" he asked.

"B, you honestly gonna sit here and act like you didn't know I liked you? That I *like* you?"

"Whoa, Tab. Are you serious right now?"

I couldn't tell if he was shocked or getting frustrated with my admission. I sat, looking down at my feet and moving the dirt around, avoiding his gaze. I could feel it burning a hole in the side of my face.

"Tab?"

"What, B?"

"What you saying, babe?"

"I'm saying that I like you, B and you up and got married on me. You didn't even call to tell me. I run into you at the gas station and you drop the bomb all matter of fact and like ..."

He cut me off, "Like you're my friend?"

"Yeah. Like I'm your damn friend or some shit." Now I was annoyed because for some reason I feel reduced to just a friend.

"Tab, you *are* my friend. I'm just now, today, hearing about how you felt o-or feel ... I should be fucking mad that you withheld that shit."

"Byron, why would you be mad?"

"Hell, maybe I wouldn't have gotten fucking married if I knew you were feeling me like that."

Wow, what an admission.

He was quiet for a bit as if he realized how jacked up his statement was. I didn't say anything because I wanted him to continue.

I looked up at him and could see him feeling something, I just didn't know what. We sat in that silence for what felt like an eternity.

"Tab, I don't just like you. I fell in love with you. I didn't think the feeling was mutual so I bounced. I couldn't just be sitting around you all the time being your friend, but wanting to kiss on you and show you some real nasty shit I think you'd like."

I chuckle a little bit, "Why didn't *you* say anything, B?"

"Hell I put myself out there all the time with you. Telling you how beautiful you are, how smart you are, and how much I admire and enjoy you. What the fuck you think I was getting at? That's how niggas say 'I love you' in the beginning. Why you think I held on so long and so tight whenever you would give me a hug?"

"Honestly, B, I just thought you were a real emotionally secure dude."

"Get the fuck outta here, Tab. You can't be this clueless, smart as you are."

I didn't know if I should have been offended or flattered. Was that what folks call a *backhanded compliment*?

"Byron, I figured that with as generous as you were with the compliments, if you wanted more, you would have just said it. After all, this whole "friendship" began with you being a man about shit. Stating your intentions and saying what you wanted."

"OK, Tab. I see we are gonna just have to agree to disagree because I don't want to waste the time I have left with you arguing."

"I agree with you on that."

We talked for about fifteen more minutes before he sent me on my way: "Hey, it's getting late and you shouldn't be out here this late ... especially with a married man."

He was obviously in his feelings, big-time.

"So you rubbing it in?"

"Naw ... just fucking with you. But yeah, go on home Tab. Call me and let me know you made it. I'll be out for a little while longer."

I agreed, hopped in my car and pulled off. I had the radio on and Gerald Levert's "Thinkin' Bout It" played. *FUCK*!

After that night, Byron continued to call and request my time. I told him that his being married changed the dynamics of our friendship and with the admission of feelings, I didn't know how to continue being his friend. I explained that while I enjoyed his attention and the talks we had, I was not interested in crossing that line. I could tell that such a boundary was far from his mind. There was a shift in his energy, I could literally feel his attraction to me. Maybe it was more obvious with the acknowledgement. His response to my suggesting some boundaries caught me off guard.

"I understand your position and respect it wholeheartedly, *but* I won't deny what I feel now that it's out in the open."

"Byron—" He cut me off.

"Tab, it is what it is. You want me to leave you alone altogether?"

The true answer was no, but that was also the inappropriate answer. Ambiguity is what I gave: "You're grown, B. You know what's best for you and your situation. You don't need me to give you permission or a denial."

Byron didn't let up on the calls and the requests for visits. He pursued me like a single and available man would. He called regularly. He met me in the park near my job, brought me lunch and never looked at his watch to acknowledge the time restraints that should exist with a married man.

Byron was affectionate and attentive. He regularly told how beautiful I was to him. He told me how he admired my natural beauty and how easy it was for him to talk to me. He complemented things about me that I had either ignored or didn't think people noticed. He told me that my brown eyes sparkle when I give a genuine smile. He told me how he loved the appearance and disappearance of my dimples when I spoke. He noticed that there are certain letters or words that allow my dimples to show more than others.

I fell for him hard and effortlessly. It was organic, slow and gradual. Often times, I forgot that he was a married man.

Byron juggled me and his wife with ease. He became more relaxed with his time with me. The secret rendezvous lunches in the park slowly turned into full lunch dates in local restaurants. He introduced me to some of his friends and family. We even went on a couple of dates to the movies. The more time we spent together, the more comfortable and relaxed we got.

Byron was a fully married man. Not separated. Married. Fully married and living with his wife while carrying out a full on relationship with me. There was no request to date me, no conversation about carrying on with this inappropriate courtship. Things just evolved.

At some point, Byron had begun taking care of me, like *really* taking care of me. He paid bills at my house. He made sure my hair and nails were done on a regular basis. He made sure that I had gas in my car at all times and that the regular maintenance was up to date. Husband-like things, for me.

With all of that pampering and care taking came gradual possessiveness. He started to voice his opinion about the partying I was doing. He wanted to approve my outfits before I went out. As time went on, he seemed to have forgotten that there was only one married person in this relationship.

I remember wondering when things changed and quickly realized that the moment we had slept together, he flipped the script. It was a damn good night.

He let his romantic side show by preparing a picnic dinner for us to have on my living room floor. He laid out a pink chenille blanket, covered with white and red rose petals. Vases of my favorite flower, tulips, in a variety of colors had adorned my living room. Candles flickered their soft glow. There was a crystal saucer with chocolate covered strawberries and champagne with strawberries drowning in the fluted glass. We dined on a chef-prepared dinner of salad, seafood pasta with the most amazing garlic rolls. A homemade strawberry cake was the dessert.

After dinner, we listened to music and talked. Lying on my back, enjoying the sounds of Maxwell singing about how *Fortunate* he was, Byron traced my nose with his pinky. He circled my eyes and my lips.

"Have I told you today how beautiful you are to me?"

"Yes sir. You tell me every day."

He leaned down and kissed me. It was soft and deliberate at first. Then he cupped my face and kissed me deeper. I let out a soft moan. Byron laid beside me and licked my neck while rubbing my thighs and pulling me into him. He rose to look at me again, "I've been wanting do that for a long time."

"Is that so," I needed to catch my breath.

"Yes. Among other things."

Confidence speaking through me, "Show me those other things."

Byron looked shocked and immediately began to undress me. After removing each article of clothing, he looked at me with a gaze of satisfaction. If that wasn't an ego boost, I don't know what would be.

No more words were spoken, just moans and groans. He took my leopard print bra off, exposing my erect nipples, and moaned. He pulled at my pants while biting his bottom lip. He groaned when my matching leopard print panties were visible. He tugged at my panties. I lifted my bottom so that he could remove them with ease. More shock in his eyes at the landing strip left on my vagina.

Byron leaned down to kiss my stomach. He traced circles around my belly button with his tongue. He nibbled on my pelvic bone. All while caressing my thighs. One of Byron's hands moved to one of my inner thighs to push open my legs. He inserted three of his fingers where I was wet. There was that sound again. The sound of sweet wetness.

Byron pushed his fingers in and out of me until that wet sound grew louder. Just as a moan broke free from my throat, he pulled his fingers from me and inserted them in his mouth. He maintained eye contact with me. Byron sucked every last drop of my essence from his fingers. Still fully clothed, he pushed my legs open wider and disappeared between them. He licked me from front to back in a long, soft stroke before slipping his tongue in the place where his fingers just were. He sucked on my labia and reinserted his fingers. That night I realized how sensitive my clitoris was. When Byron flicked his tongue on it as fast as a hummingbird's wings, it sent shockwaves through my body. I could hardly stand it. There were so many sensations at one time. When Byron felt my body stiffen, he removed his fingers and allowed his tongue to lap up what was to come. I exploded in his mouth and it was *the* most intense feeling I had ever felt in my life. There was wetness beneath me. The pretty chenille blanket soaked. Byron rose to remove his pants and quickly inserted his penis inside of me while I was still writhing with pleasure. That insertion magnified my satisfaction and my extremities lost blood again. Energy was building again.

Byron moved in and out of me slowly and deeply. Moaning. Groaning and the occasional *oh shit!* I could tell that his energy was mounting by the intensity of his movements. Our passions released simultaneously. My release slightly less intense than the first, but still satisfactory.

I could feel his manhood pulsating inside of me. He didn't pull out immediately. I supposed he wanted to give me every last drop, especially since he hadn't worn a condom. We slept on the floor of my living room, naked and surrounded by rose petals, many of which were stuck to our bodies.

Awoken by the sunrise, I suddenly realized that this married man had spent the night with me.

"Byron! It's morning!" I jumped up, frantic.

He groaned and rolled over, rose petals on his ass.

"Byron, you spent the night!" Still nothing from him. *Why was I the one in a panic when I was where I was supposed to be?* I thought.

I got up to clean the area.

"You drained me. I've never had sex so good" said the *married* man.

"Wow, B. What does that say about your wife?"

"That you're better than her in bed ... well on the floor. Seeing as how we never made it to the bed." He laughed at his own joke and began to pick up the remaining rose petals that he was lying on. "The whole rose petals idea is cute and shit, until you have to clean these motherfuckers up."

I paused from tidying up the area of our date, "B, I have a question."

"Yep." He said without looking up at me.

I appreciated his willingness to help me clean up without my having to ask. With an empty wine bottle in one hand and wine glasses in the other, I sat down on the arm of my sofa. "Where does your wife think you are?"

He sighed, "Tab, let me worry about her."

Irritated by his attempt to evade the question, "Naw, B, how are you not tripping about having spent the night here?"

He sat on the sofa next to me. He looked up at me and said, "I'm in the deer woods as far as she's concerned. Hunting all weekend."

"Ok, so are you headed to the deer woods when you leave here?"

"I am. I'll be back Monday morning. You'll be good until then, right?" He said with a grin.

"As good as a single chick can be." I replied knowing he caught the underlying jab.

Byron's possessiveness did not involve violence and he rarely got angry with my defiance to his requests. He was never mean to me, but it was very clear that he didn't want me to entertain any other man, despite him going home to his wife every night. Byron didn't understand that companionship is much more than providing. I wanted him to understand that I missed my friend. I missed the companionship that I had with him.

As juggling two households and two women became another full time job, things continued to evolve with us. He had less time to hang out with me as his wife became more demanding of his time or with knowing his whereabouts. Talking on the phone after a 8 p.m. was no longer an option.

Since I was spending less time with Byron, I began to spend more time out with my friends. He didn't like that. His expectation was that if he couldn't be in my presence, he needed to be able to have phone contact with me; all of this was on his terms.

In the first years of knowing Byron, even with the frequent pauses in our communication, I had enjoyed the friendship that we built. I had allowed myself to engage in this affair because at our base level, we were great friends. I valued his take on life and he enjoyed experiencing college life vicariously through me.

The change and the rules made things less fun for me. The spontaneity had dwindled. The dates and meet-ups became more clandestine. Phone calls became rushed. This was no longer fun.

In the last year of Byron and my escapade, after I had joined my sorority, I requested to meet up with Byron following my initiation ceremony. It was a Sunday and I was 45 minutes away. I thought this would be the perfect opportunity to meet up in a neutral place without fear of being seen. Byron had arrived at the meeting spot before me and was in his brother's truck. My palms were sweaty and I was nervous about what I called the meeting to do. It was time to go our separate ways. For good.

As if he sensed that something was up, Byron hopped out of the truck and ran to my side.

"Tab, you good? Is everything ok?" There was such concern in his voice.

I managed a half smile. My stomach was in knots. "I'm good B. Just needed to talk to you a bit and thought it best to speak in person."

He escorted me to the huge truck and helped me inside. It smelled of cherries. Byron was back in the driver's seat before I could collect my thoughts.

"Ok, Tab. What's up?" Such concern in his voice. It almost sounded like worry.

"I-I ..." Byron cut me off.

"Are you pregnant?" Now, that question sounded like excitement, which was concerning considering the circumstances.

"Hell no." That slipped out and sounded more harsh than I intended. I continued, "Byron. I can't do this anymore. This whole situation isn't fun for me anymore. I was so wrapped up in the fantasy of things that I had completely abandoned all reason."

"You starting to feel bad?"

"B, I been feeling bad. I just don't want to feel this anymore. I want my own man, and I can't make room for that as long as you're in the picture."

There was a long pause. Byron shifted in his seat and looked straight ahead for what felt like an eternity. I wanted to continue because the silence was painful. I wanted to know what was going on in his head. Instead, I sat in the stillness.

My gaze moving back and forth between the sun setting in the distance and Byron. The sunset was almost symbolic. Like it was setting on a relationship that spanned five years from that day I met him at the department store. I reached for his hand. He gave it to me and looked in my eyes. His eyes looked glassy. They looked like mine felt as the tears began to well up.

"I get it Tab. You're a beautiful, smart woman inside and out and I can't be so selfish anymore. I knew it were only a matter of time that you'd want more. I knew when we started this here that there was an expiration date and I knew that it would be your call. Hell, if it were up to me, I would find a way to maintain two families," Byron half joked in what I assumed was an attempt to lighten the mood. There was a lump in my throat. He was handling the talk a lot better than I had anticipated. Byron smiled and let out a deep sigh, "Shit, Tab."

I had no words to comfort him. None to comfort myself. This was tough because ending this affair also felt like losing a friend. I couldn't have one without the other. I leaned over and kissed him on the cheek.

Byron was still holding my hand. He tightened his grip as I pulled away from him. "I love you, Tab. Always will."

I gave a tight lipped smile and reached for the door handle. Byron reluctantly let my hand go and I jumped out of the big truck. Tears fell as I walked slowly to my car facing the sunset. The sky a baby blue and orange glow. I drove home in silence. No music. Just my thoughts of already missing my friend turned lover. The weights of guilt and shame not as heavy. Alone with just my thoughts. Thoughts that I would somehow pay for having an affair with a married man.

When I arrived to my apartment it was eerily quiet. I felt exhausted. Physically and mentally. My mind was busy. I showered and poured myself a glass of wine. I laid across the top of my bed enveloped in silence. Alone with my thoughts.

I drifted into a daydream. I imagined Karma as a person. A beautiful woman. She had gorgeous olive skin and dark thick hair in a big top knot. She had on a black fitted t-shirt that read *what goes around, comes around*. She sat at the foot of my bed and watched me.

I watched her. Amazed by her beauty, I watched. Her softness. She didn't seem like a bitch at all. Her lips didn't move, but I heard: *You're not marriage material, you just get them ready for other women*; *You know you're reaping what you've sown, right*; *You shouldn't have messed with a married man, you'll never have your own man.*

While the words were harsh. Karma's eyes were soft. On some level I felt I deserved every one of the negative words. I wondered if they were my own thoughts or if she somehow implanted her thoughts in my mind. I felt comforted by Karma's loving gaze.

I cried a cleansing cry. I asked Karma to release me from Byron and to help him to let go of me too. She nodded and as quickly as she had appeared, she was gone.

Lesson 8: Therapy

I wake up angry. Tension in my neck and shoulders make it uncomfortable to experience a full range of motion with my head. I lie in the bed trying to remember why I feel like I was just run over by a Mack truck. My mood is funky and I feel like complete shit. Nothing registers right away, but I need to change my mood quickly.

"Alexa, play 'Real Love' by Mary J. Blige," I command. I need something to get my day going in a better direction. I don't want to travel in a bad mood. I sing and dance around the condo gathering my things while attempting to lift my mood.

I check my planner to remind myself of the plans I have scheduled for the week in an attempt to shift my mind. *Could my sour mood and built up tension be because my short retreat has come to an end?*

As this thought comes to mind, Mary sings about trying her best and praying to God that He sends her someone real. Then it hit me. This retreat has been emotional. While it was a release to go through my mental Rolodex of relationships, I suppose I hadn't realized the impact that I still carry from those situations. I count my tears as a cleanse, but I still need to fully grasp what the release actually means. I have an appointment with Dr. Drea today when I land. It will be well spent on fully processing the things that have resurfaced during my time of reflection.

The tension lingers, thicker in my shoulders than my neck. I do a little yoga on the beach before I head to the airport. The morning is cool and the dawn sky is beautiful. The sun just peeking over the sea miles away, not so bright that I can't look directly at it. The wispy clouds are painted on a canvas of baby blue and shades of pink that blend to a perfect lavender.

I take a moment and allow my entire body to feel gratitude for this sunrise and the for even waking up on my own accord. I start with breaths and head rotations. Deep breath in, exhale a slow *thank you*. I proceed with a short Vinyasa routine and sit in the sand to watch the sun fully grace us with its full glory. While my tension is still present, my mood has greatly improved.

Home sweet home. My trip home was smooth and uneventful. I arrive thirty minutes ahead of schedule. Rather than calling anyone to pick me up, I call an Uber. I don't feel like speaking about my trip to anyone but Dr. Drea.

Walking into my home, I release things. Shoes off at the door. My suitcase and my bag on the couch. I unbutton my denim shirt dress and call out, "Alexa, shuffle Homebody playlist." The first song up is "Charlene" by Anthony Hamilton.

I sway my way to my bedroom to start the shower. "Woke this morning ... " I begin to sing along. My phone rings, but I ignore it. My therapy appointment is in 45 minutes and no one will get the details before I have a chance to go over them with my therapist.

"Baby I'll be sitting here waiting ... "

I find a comfortable outfit to put on and lay it on the bed. I continue to sing around my room.

"... promise I'll be here till the very end ..."

I take my time in the shower while considering all that I will share with Dr. Drea. Where to start and where to end.

As I get out of the shower, I harmonize with Lauryn Hill: "dooo oooh oooh, oooh oooh oooh, oooh oooh oooh. Oooh oooh oooh. Oooh oooh oooh, oooh oooh oooh ..." before Nas chimes in with "Life ..." and check my phone. Three missed calls. One from my mom, one from Chaz, and one from my cousin Crystal. *They'll have to wait* I think to myself.

I tune back in to the music and my thoughts. Music has always helped me process things. I bop around the room, back and forth from the bathroom to my closet, singing about what I'd do *If I Ruled the World*. I continue my little concert in my car, singing along to Tyrese's "Sweet Lady."

In and out of awareness of the song, I am lining out my portion of my session. Considering what I'll reveal today and what I'll hold on to for a little while, all the while knowing that it'll never go as I plan. Dr. Drea has a way of pulling shit out of me. Things that I hadn't really thought through fully will end up spilled on her chevron patterned rug. I pull up at the office just as Mariah Carey begins to share her "Vision of Love." I briefly consider sitting in the car to finish the song, but by then I'd be late.

I gather my notebook, full of notes taken on my trip. Talking points that I want to process with Dr. Drea. I walk into the office and notice that there is a small can of cherry coke sitting on the table next to my place on Dr. Drea's couch. There is soft meditation music playing. Music less likely to cause another emotional response in me. I smirk at the thought, slightly embarrassed by how I acted during the session before my trip. I imagine that I must have seemed like a complete nut case to her. I'm also sure that she's used to it.

Dr. Drea interrupts my thoughts. "Hey Tabitha! How are you?"

"Hey Doc. Thanks for the soda. I'm doing well." I pop open the can and take a swig.

"So catch me up. What's been going on since we last met?"

I adjust my posture to get more comfortable. I open my notebook, "Well after our last session, I decided to take a trip to my family's beach house. I gathered some of my old journals and had a healing retreat of sorts."

"Oh wow." Dr. Drea looks intrigued. "So tell me about it." She jumps right in.

"I um. Uh, I don't know where to start really." I thought I was prepared. Such open ended questions always stump me.

"How about we start with this morning and work our way back?"

Not at all surprised that she'd have a solution I begin, "Well I woke with an attitude. Angry. I sat with that and spent time trying to figure out why I woke so discontent. I watched the sunrise while doing Vinyasa Yoga and that helped. I came to the conclusion at that time that I was irritated because my trip was at its end, but that didn't seem to resolve the feelings of frustration."

"Ok, did something else come up for you?"

"I kept going back to the feelings I had at the very start of my day and my reasoning for it, and the more that reason didn't feel to resonate, the more I pondered the thoughts." I'm still trying to grasp the words. The right description. The culprit for the feelings. "I-I just wonder if it is more than the fact that the trip was over."

"Ok, well what about your last night? How was that?"

"So I took old journals with the idea that I would read about the younger me and past experiences in an attempt to gain insight about repeating patterns. I went back to when I was sixteen and read about the pivotal moments of that year. It sucked. Then I went to my first real relationship. That sucked too. Then my second relationship, which sucked even more. Then I had two not so sucky situations that hurt equally as bad."

"Tabitha, what does any of that mean?"

I sigh. The thought of rehashing the situations is causing a fire to bubble in the pit of my stomach. I know that this is what I came to do. To process all the stuff that resurfaced for me, but I'm kind of having second thoughts. It feels like I am about to scratch up a scab. Maybe this is why I felt so irritated this morning. The thought of having to regurgitate all the crap that came up over the weekend. I take a deep breath and adjust my posture. It's about to get real. I decide to give her my assessment of who I was then and what lessons I learned at that time.

"Dr. Drea, the short of it all is that I was almost a hoe, I suffered from low self-esteem and was very impressionable. I found it difficult to say no, even in situations that I was not cool with. I put up with bullshit and settled for unavailable men, all the while allowing a decent man to slip through my fingers. My judgement was crap, and I still see remnants of that now, nearly two decades later. If I'm completely honest, I'm still doing the same shit."

Dr. Drea nods and writes on her pad. She uses therapeutic silence like a secret weapon. I attempt to wait her out. It doesn't work.

"I found myself emotional about my naivety and lack of voice. I suppose I was angry that no one taught me better. Angry that I had to learn lessons from experiences. Lessons that left scars that I'm still trying to heal." I fight hard to hold back, but tears flow. I look at the time and I hit a new record, in tears less than 20 minutes into the session.

"So what did you learn at that time and what did you learn looking back?"

I move my eyes from the pretty clock on the wall. I never really looked at it before. I take a deep breath to allow myself a moment to collect my composure. "I learned then that I put up with the dumbest shit because I didn't want to hurt anyone's feelings or didn't want anyone mad at me. Looking back on those experience revealed that I still shrink and stifle my voice sometimes, but not out of fear of someone being upset with me." I pause to carefully consider the why, "I shrink for fear of what people will *think* about me." *Damn.* "I have not consistently lived authentically."

"Wow, Tabitha, that's good stuff. I hear what you're saying about the pain you endured and why. I can see how, at times, you continue that cycle. The comforts of habits, no matter how unhelpful, are hard to break. How do you get off the merry-go-round?"

"I don't know, Doc. I was hoping you'd tell me," I admit.

"Well, first, let's not use the crutch of 'I don't know.' That's what we say when we don't want to think or dig deep. How do those past experiences show up in your life today?"

I take a moment to consider my response. To really allow the question to soak in my mind. "Well, I don't do this as much anymore, but for years after losing my virginity I felt obligated to have sex with a guy if I helped get him aroused. I somehow felt responsible for his arousal. I didn't want to be labeled a tease and have the guy upset with me. Now, we won't even get to the opportunity of arousal if I'm not feeling him. I have become more comfortable with setting boundaries to prevent the feeling of obligation. The thing is Doc, I don't think that change was the result of a particular lesson or past experience, I think that just came with maturity." I take a moment to think. "There are just so many more experiences and so many more lessons that I need to uncover."

"Then let's do that Tabitha. Tell me this, in all of your reflecting, did you remember anything positive?"

"Oh yes. There was Troy. Reading the journal entries about him was a more pleasant walk down memory lane. I liked him and I believe he liked me. He was respectful, didn't pressure me to have sex, and was a lot of fun. I recall good interactions with him." I smile at the memories. For a moment I allow the recollection of that time to resurface. Looking at the wall, at nothing in particular, I remember Troy.

Dr. Drea breaks my trance, "OK? What happened there? What lesson did you learn there?"

With a deep sigh, I explain, "I let him slip through my fingers by giving my loyalty to someone undeserving. At the time, I thought that it was right to be a faithful chick. I didn't really consider my own needs. I basically kicked my own ass for letting him get away."

"Could it be that you weren't really ready for Troy at that time?"

I nod in agreement. "Hindsight being 20/20, I suppose I wasn't. I was still learning what I liked and didn't really know who I was. I needed to develop some self-awareness, which was missing back then. I was barely legal and had only had two failed relationships. Hadn't experienced enough at that time. I realize now that while I don't believe that I need to be 100% healed, I do need to at least have a good idea of who I am."

"Good insight, Tabitha."

I sit in the silence again, pondering the lessons I continue to learn. Reading through the journals will become more difficult. Examining those situations against my current interactions will require the insight that Dr. Drea says I have if I am to move forward in a different way.

"What are you thinking?" Dr. Drea asks. I return my focus to this session and her face.

"About the next phase of my relationships and the lessons from those. I can't take another trip and I have several more journals to get through," I answered.

"You can do that work right here in the city. Read and reflect a little bit every night. Use your sessions to fully process them as you did today. We can meet as often as you want until we work through every relationship that you feel significantly impacted you."

I agree. Dr. Drea pencils me in to return in two weeks. I finish my soda and walk slowly out of her office.

I'm hesitant to rush home because I know exactly where I will pick up. *This is gonna be a tough two weeks*, I think to myself. Reggie is up next and I really need an entire appointment to unpack that one. I pick up a salad and head home.

Once home, I settle into bed and pull out my current journal. I record my thoughts and feelings after my session.

I am reluctant to continue this exercise because of the emotions that I know will come up and the hard truths I will have to face. I know that I play a role in my own heartbreak, I can acknowledge that. Admitting that to someone else is a different story. I don't want to feel regret. I don't want to feel stupid. Even more, I don't want to repeat the cycle.

I sit in my own silence and remind myself aloud of the cliché saying, "The only way to it, is through it." Well here goes, I open the red leather bound journal and search for Reggie's story.

Lesson 9: Reggie

Chaz is my oldest friend. My sorority sister. A true ride or die. She's a couple of years older than me, but we connect so well. We don't judge each other and never asked about what happened behind closed doors during our college partying days. We have a level of respect and understanding that surpasses most sister-friendships. Chaz is NOT the friend you call to bail you out of jail for vandalizing your boyfriend's car. She is the friend who paid cash for the spray paint, drove you 60 miles in her uncle's car to help you paint obscene words on your boyfriend's brand new Mustang. And while sitting in jail trying to figure out who can bail you both out asks, "Girl what he do"? She gives "ride or die" a whole new meaning.

Much of my college time is a blur, but Chaz was clearly a part of it. On a Saturday shopping trip, likely buying outfits to wear out to a party, a guy coming out of Footlocker caught my eye as Chaz and I walked by the store. His swag on a level that I can't describe, caused an immediate attraction. I stopped mid-sentence of something I was telling Chaz.

I remember that day, or at least the part of me seeing this guy, vividly. He wore camouflage cargo shorts, a white tee shirt, all white Air Max 90s and a rugged khaki hat with large fishing hooks in it. It was as if time moved in slow motion just like in the movies.

Our eyes connected, he said "hello" and I got a whiff of his cologne. Chaz nudged me with her elbow as if to tell me to speak. I said "hello," but continued walking. I tried to play it cool. He grabbed my hand and motioned for me to come to him. I could see the bright green Extra gum in his mouth.

I could have fallen to the floor. I loved everything about him instantly. The way he dressed, the way he smelled, his smooth and confident movements. His hands were even soft. His name was Reggie and he had a smile that looked like his parents had paid a lot of money to ensure that Colgate grin. He had my full attention from the moment we locked eyes.

We exchanged numbers that day in the mall and spoke daily for three months straight. We had completely opposite schedules and he lived 25 miles away from me, so we had to get creative with how we spent time together. Though my initial attraction to him was purely carnal, as I got to know him, it became more than that for me. I genuinely enjoyed him. He made me laugh. The snorting, embarrassing kind of laugh. Chaz would ride with me on nights that I would drive to his area for a visit. She ultimately started dating one of his friends, the four of us had lots of good times. Occasionally he made the 25 mile trek to my apartment. Six weeks in and no sex, the temptation was building as fast as the chemistry.

One cool fall night he decided that he would rather come see me than go to work. I grinned from ear to ear as he made the confession. I, of course, consented to the idea and began tidying-up my apartment. It wasn't nasty, just cluttered in some places, namely my desk. I was a college student after all. I neatly stacked textbooks in one place, and the two novels I was reading in another. I put away my pens, pencils, and note cards and for a moment considered leaving them out. I over prepared to welcome him into my home.

I took a nice hot shower and dressed in a college tee shirt and warm ups, no underwear. Reggie arrived an hour later with my favorite snacks. Impressed, I let out a squeal and gave him a sincere hug. He had to go out of his way to get these snacks. He brought me Cherry Heads, Cheetos hot fries, and a strawberry-kiwi Snapple. Unless you lived in the hood, you wouldn't find all three of these in the same place, maybe two of the three, but not the jackpot of all three. I loved him for this.

Then I noticed that he too is sporting a college tee shirt and basketball shorts. Reggie whipped out another surprise. He brought the DVD of *Richard Pryor: Live and Smokin'*. This man surely knew how to wow me. Favorite snacks and guaranteed laughs was my kind of night.

Apparently laughing was a turn on for Reggie because as soon as the DVD started, so did he. It began with light, barely-there touches up and down my arms as I sat cross legged between his legs, my back against his chest. We shared hot fries, but only if I fed them to him. Two for me, three for him. He made sure to lick my fingers before I could pull them away. It was a gradual build to arousal, rising slowly like the climax of a good movie.

More laughs, more fries, a few sips of Snapple and those barely there touches that turned into full caresses of my arm. The touches moved to my leg. We were still fully dressed, but that would not be the case at the conclusion of Richard's jokes. More laughs, more hot fries, light kisses on the neck. My body made involuntary movements. I shifted my position so that Reggie could have good access to my neck. Then I lay between Reggie's legs with an open mouth and the low moans escaped. As the jokes continued and the caresses increased, my tee shirt was moved above my waist and Reggie had full access to my stomach and breasts.

I put the snacks on the coffee table to free up my hands so that I could trace the paths of Reggie's hands on my body with my own hands. Richard continued to make the audience in New York scream with laughter. I could hear him faintly tell a joke about drugs, but it was harder to hear him with the heavy breathing, the loud swooshing in my ears, my blood was flowing to areas that helped Reggie get me to the optimal state of arousal.

We never discussed anything sexual, it was just implied through our interactions that there was good chemistry and sexual tension present. Reggie didn't brag about his abilities. He never told me what he wanted or would do to my body if given the opportunity. I could tell that he had every intention on showing me that night much better than he could ever tell me.

We moved to the floor, right in front of the TV. Somehow we managed to do that seamlessly without standing. It was a smooth slide from my sofa to my floor, Reggie never taking a hand from my body. Still fully dressed, I felt his manhood perfectly. It made me a little nervous. I assumed he knew what to do with all of that. I hoped he'd be gentle with me.

While I was all in my head about the possibilities and whether or not I would enjoy it, Reggie turned me over and I felt him tugging at my shirt. I lifted up to allow him to take it off. He looked at me, my body, my bare breasts, smiled and moved closer to kiss me again. Oh how I loved kissing that man. It was almost otherworldly. The effect that his kisses had on my entire body was amazing.

I took off his shirt. He wasn't chiseled, but I liked what I saw nonetheless. I rubbed my hands up and down his torso, he played in my hair. Those small intimate touches helped to build to an imminent explosive release of tension. Reggie bent to kiss my stomach, he let his tongue linger in my navel. He nibbled on my hips as he pulled my pants down. The look of surprise as he saw that I had no panties on, was priceless.

I suppose one surprise deserved another because Reggie spread my legs, kissed my thighs and licked my center from back to front. I grabbed his head in shock, but not in a way that signaled that I wanted him to stop. He seemed to enjoy tasting every drop I had to give. *Get out of your head. Get out of your head*, I thought so that I could fully be in the moment, enjoying the feelings rather than analyzing the act. Reggie sucked and licked while massaging my breasts. I forgot to breathe, and when I did allow the automatic bodily function to resume, I relaxed into him.

More involuntary body action, I began to move my pelvis to the rhythm of his tongue movements. As if to read the responses that my body sent, Reggie amplified his technique. It felt as if he had two tongues. As his methods intensified, my movements responded accordingly. The slow build started in my toes and fingertips. Energy moved from my extremities to meet at my core. My breathing labored, my eyes closed, I relaxed completely.

I was no longer touching him. I was no longer on a hard floor. It felt like I was on a cloud, I heard nothing. Richard's jokes faded. It was like I was under water. I just felt Reggie performing cunnilingus like a professional in the Olympics; and he was going for the gold. I don't know how long he was down there, but it was obvious that he had no plans of getting up until he had reached his goal. The closer I got to climax, the more intense his focus.

As my body relaxed more, I heard *and* felt a strong vibration. Reggie let out a moan that vibrated from the depths of his being and shook mine. With his nose up against my clitoris, my tender spot was stimulated by the reverberation of his own pleasure and that did it. I stiffened. My thighs tightened around his head. We had lift off. He wasn't done, he continued. Reggie licked my sweet spot until he had gotten every last drop.

I begged him to stop. The intensity I felt was too strong. I was out of breath. He had mercy and acknowledged my tapping out. Reggie kissed the inside of my thighs, my clitoris and the spot he had just savored. My sweet spot received the best kiss of her life, of my life.

Reggie's goatee glistened as he removed his own pants. I didn't move. I couldn't move. My legs remained open, waiting for the next treat. He delicately touched my body and I fluttered. He smiled and slowly kissed my breasts and then my neck.

He raised his head to my ear and whispered, "you taste good."

Before I could respond and with his lips touching my ear, he inserted his rock hard erection in my pool of moisture. "Oh my," was all I could utter.

Reggie was slow and methodical. He didn't speak, but his nonverbal communication was loud and clear. His eyes were closed and every so often he let out a guttural moan. Slow and methodical, balanced on one arm so as not to put all of his weight on me. Sweet kisses planted on my neck as he moved smoothly against me. His moves were measured and intense, he knew exactly what he was doing.

I kissed his shoulder, then his neck. I ran my fingertips lightly up and down his back, he liked that. I pulled him closer to me so that my low moans could waft softly to his ear without a problem. His movements sped up and he groaned deeper, louder. This dance intensified, somehow while Reggie pressed in and out of me, he managed to rub against my clitoris. The build began again, leaving my toes and fingertips without feeling.

Reggie moved faster. His moans mixed with mine. He rose higher above me, placed my ankles on his shoulders for better leverage as he moved faster and harder. He kissed my feet one at a time, literally leaving nothing untouched by his tongue. I relaxed again, merged with the floor. Reggie moved closer to my body, lowering so he could whisper in my ear, his movements steady. My thighs pushed against my stomach, feet still on his shoulders.

"Are you gonna give me another one?" he asked.

I said nothing. He realized that I was at the brink of yet another pleasurable release. And almost simultaneously, we peaked. For me, it wasn't as intense, but great nonetheless. Reggie collapsed next to me, one hand remained on my thigh.

He mumbled a winded, "Damn."

I guess that's a good thing. We lay on the floor for a little while, not speaking; Reggie traced circles on my thigh. The TV screen was blue, the DVD had long since stopped.

"I'm cold," I said. Reggie rubbed my body in an attempt to warm me. "Are you staying over?"

He asked, "Do you mind?"

I got up and reached for his hand to lead him to my bed. He followed and watched me as I pulled the comforter back for us to climb in.

"Let's hop in the shower to clean up first."

"Together?" I asked.

He approached me with a sly smile, standing an entire foot taller than I and replied, "Yes."

I agreed and for the first time ever, I took a shower with a man.

We slept naked: another first for me. Reggie made me feel good about my body. The way he touched me in both sexual and nonsexual ways, the way he looked at me, it all signaled that he saw nothing wrong. I liked that.

I woke before he did the morning after. I brushed my teeth, ran a comb through my tangled hair and put on a clean tee shirt. While Reggie slept, I gathered the remnants of the snacking from the night before and picked the sofa pillows up from the floor.

I was in my own world tidying up my place for the second time in less that 12 hours while reminiscing on how good Reggie made me feel just hours earlier. I didn't hear or notice him enter the living room. He was fully dressed, with his underwear in his hand. He looked like he slept well, his puffy eyes made him look innocent, but I knew better. My body know better. Reggie was not innocent.

"I gotta go ... don't want to go, but I have to."

I smiled, "I understand. I had a great evening with you and I'm glad you ditched work for me. I feel all special and shit. You really showed me some things."

He replied, "It was well worth it. When can I see you again?"

I played coy. "Just let me know when and we will see how to make it work."

He agreed, kissed my forehead and I walked him to the door. I climbed back in bed, quivered at every memory of last night. I smiled to myself and drifted off in to a daydream.

It had been two weeks since my Richard Pryor night with Reggie. We continued to talk almost daily, but our schedules were crazy. The beginning of the semester was always super busy. Chaz and I were making plans for a girl's night at her house for her birthday. She said just a few ladies were plenty.

I was in charge of drinks. While I didn't drink but three core adult beverages, I liked knowing how to mix them for others. I often considered going to bartending school for more technical knowledge and building a side hustle. I brought what I called the Core Four, vodka, rum, tequila, and whiskey. I had mixers and wine, sodas and juices. It looked like a mobile bar.

Chaz had a table set up in front of the patio window, there was a black tablecloth with pink cups and black cocktail napkins. Shavonne brought food (wings and dips) and Crystal brought decor (balloons and party hats). After we set up, Chaz surprised us with gift bags filled with footed pajamas that matched our personalities. Chaz's pj's had lips all over them, mine martini glasses, Shavonne's were covered with coffee mugs, and Crystal's pj's were covered with unicorns. We changed while Chaz was in the living room playing DJ. "Ambitionz Az A Ridah" was playing as we made our way back to fill our cups and plates. That was my cue to start tending the bar. As I made Chaz a Cîroc and cranberry, my cellphone began to vibrate. It was Reggie.

"Hello?"

"Well hello, beautiful. What you got going on tonight? Sounds like a party."

"It's girl's night in at Chaz's place. We are celebrating her birthday."

"I was hoping to see you tonight after work."

I tried not to sound as excited as I was. "What time you get off?"

"Eleven. Is that too late?"

"No, we will still be up I'm sure."

"Honestly, I'm not really trying to see a 'we,' I only want to see you!"

Well damn, I thought, "Ok?"

"If your girls are still up after my shower, we can sneak off someplace else for a bit. Maybe go back to your crib."

"And if they aren't up?" I asked, curious about his suggestion in that scenario.

"We can chill right where you are. Look, babygirl, I just want to see your face. Kiss on you a little bit. We'll keep it PG, save the rated R shit for when I get you all to myself."

I don't know how he did it, but he made me squirm and throb at the mere thought of his plan. "Ok, Ok. Well c'mon, baby"

Reggie laughed, "Are you drinking?"

"I am."

"Don't get shit faced now, I want you fully aware for my kisses."

"Oh I'm sure regardless, I will be fully aware of anything you do." The flirting never got old.

"Ok, beautiful. I get off at eleven, will go home to shower and head your way. I expect to get there no later than one."

"Ok", I said without trying to sound as excited as I felt. We discontinued the call and I resumed my bartending duties.

We ladies drank, danced and sang 90s R&B most of the night. It was a good time. We talked about men, school, and work. We vented and got shit off of our chests. Blackstreet's "No Diggity" started and we all got up to sing along and dance.

I maintained my two drink max, especially since I was expecting Reggie. Evidently my friends needed a drink maximum as well, since they were all well inebriated by midnight. When Chaz began to slur her words, I called Reggie for an ETA. It was just a matter of time before they were all out like a light. Chaz was my gauge because she usually could hang the longest and trying to keep up with her was futile. I had a nice buzz, two glasses of wine did it for me.

"Hey babe, just checking in. These ladies are just about out, so we will be kissing on each other here."

"I'm en-route, about twenty more minutes. You need anything?"

"Naw we have all sorts of crap here. I just need you!"

"A'ight! Keep flirting with me and you gonna get fucked with your girls in the next room."

"Ooooh, don't threaten me with a good time." We both laughed and hung up.

True to form and as predicted, the party animals were knocked out for 20 minutes by the time Reggie arrived. He called to tell me that he was outside so that I could open the door. There were cups and crumpled cocktail napkins all over the place. I didn't take the time to tidy the place, he knew we were having a good time.

The girls were lying wherever they closed their eyes. Chaz was sprawled on the sofa, Shavonne was in the oversized chair with her feet on the ottoman, and Crystal was lying in the floor with a throw blanket rolled up under her head. Lucky for Reggie, he didn't have to step over anyone. He entered the condo and quietly laughed at the sight.

"Party ended kind of early, huh," he joked.

I attempted to lead him to the guest bedroom just past the living room, but there was resistance.

"I just wanted to see your pretty face and tell you that I can't stop thinking of you," he whispered.

"How sweet, but I know you didn't drive all this way just for that," I replied.

Reggie looked perplexed and asked, "What do you think I came for?"

"Where my kisses? Make this drive worth your travels."

He smiled and said, "Seeing your face *is* worth my travels. But if babygirl wants kisses, she shall have kisses."

I stopped arguing and took the compliment and all the good feelings it brought me. I pulled him again to follow me to the guest room, and again I was met with resistance. I asked, "What's wrong now?"

Reggie had a sly look in his eye and bit his bottom lip. He looked me up and down and pulled me to him. In the middle of the living room, surrounded by my drunk, passed out friends, he showed me how he missed me with a deep kiss. I tasted the Extra gum that he chews and let out a slow moan. He led me to the kitchen instead. Reggie unzipped my footed pj's and pulled them off my shoulders, he kissed each one ever so lightly. He traced little circles with his tongue before kissing my neck. He nibbled on my earlobe before telling me, "I've been craving you."

I managed a pressured, "Oh yeah," to which he responded with a moan.

He pulled my pajamas down to my waist and moved my bra strap enough to easily expose one of my breasts. He took my entire breast into his mouth as he slipped his strong, soft hand between my legs. I wrapped my arms around his neck as he whispered in my ear, "Hold on tight."

I did as commanded and he lifted me up to the counter, still with one hand between my legs and the other gripping one of my legs. On my way up, my pj's dropped to the floor exposing my black lace panties. Reggie smiled at his accomplishment, pulled back to look at me sitting on my friend's kitchen counter in my bra and panties.

It was dark, with the exception of the lights from the kitchen appliances. Reggie knew exactly where to find what he came for and he wasted no time getting to it. He returned to my lips. Planted soft pecks as he removed my panties.

I braced myself for insertion, but it didn't come. Instead, Reggie dropped to his knees and blew his warm breath on my flower. He kissed me there and licked multiple times as if to get me wet, but I didn't need any help with that. He went in and dined as if it were his first time. I reached for the wall to brace myself—this was different than two weeks ago. It was almost ravenous, but I liked it.

I tried hard not to moan too loudly, my friends were just a few feet away. Reggie inserted two fingers while softly licking my clitoris, I jerked and he wrapped one arm around my waist as if to immobilize me. My feet rested on his shoulders. Three fingers in and a sweeping motion of his tongue all around my labia, I hit my head on the cabinets and pulled his head into me. My mouth opened, I wanted to moan, but I remembered to breathe and enjoy quietly.

I wanted to move my hips to the rhythm that he set, but I also wanted to stay off the floor. I carefully moved into his face anyway. Reggie had me completely stabilized so I wouldn't fall, I continued to move into his face as he licked and sucked and pushed his fingers in and out of me. The slow build started, hands and feet tingled and the energy moved to the center of my body. I stopped moving, I relaxed.

My hands fell from the wall and from Reggie's head. He knew what was coming, he knew that I was cumming. He read my body so well. I shifted. He shifted too. He moved his arm from my waist to cup my breast. The fingers once going in and out of me moved to my thigh. He moaned, sending vibrations from his nose to my swollen clit causing an intense sensation that mixed pleasure with slight pain, it was a fierce feeling. One that he did well.

It was quiet. I was floating on that cloud I enjoyed. I stiffened. My legs tightened around his head and an involuntary moan escaped my lungs as air was forced out. Reggie covered my mouth, he preferred to silence my moans over stopping. And once again, he left no drop wasted. I released his head from my thighs. I felt weak. It was euphoric. Reggie stood with a full erection and I anticipated the main course. I wiped his mouth and kissed him, we both attempted to speak between pants.

I managed a winded, "Damn."

"Did you enjoy that?"

"Hell yes, I did," I said breathing as if I had run a mile.

He replied, "Good, now I have to go."

My mouth dropped open and I struggled to find the words needed that would have expressed my disappointment.

He explained, "You were loud, my dear, and I don't want to be here when your girls wake."

I couldn't argue and he made his way to the door. I slipped my pj's back up and grabbed my panties to catch up with him. He bent to kiss me and opened the door.

"Call me when you wake." He flashed me a sly smile and walked out.

And just like that, my pleasure provider was gone. My girls still asleep, unaware of the pleasure that was provided mere feet from them.

One Friday night, about a month after the girls night, Reggie called to tell me that he secured a private spot for us to hang out and shoot a little pool. He didn't say exactly where I would be meeting him, just provided an address and it was up to old Garmin to get me there.

I drove for thirty minutes to what looked like the country. I pulled onto a gravel drive surrounded by lots of old, oak trees that I imagine held a lot of secrets. At the end there was a beautiful log cabin and Reggie was leaning against his white Chevy Camaro.

He walked over to my car and opened my door, greeted me with a longing hug and said, "I've missed your face." For a month we had been talking about hanging out again, but our schedules proved that to be more difficult than we preferred. When Reggie called to say tonight's the night, I jumped at the chance.

We walk to the door hand in hand. It was a nice cozy spot. Black and red flannel rugs covered parts of the hardwood floors. The interior was dimly lit by low wattage lamps and candles here and there. The smell of warm apple pie seemed so fitting for a cabin. Reggie led me to a room in the back. There were wings and wine waiting on the pool table.

I asked, "Will it just be the two of us?"

He replied, "Of course, when I get time with you, I want you all to myself."

I blushed. I loved compliments and Reggie was not selfish with them. We ate, laughed, drank and talked. It was a very laid back evening. After eating, we played a little pool, showing our competitive sides. After losing to him twice, I was done. It was embarrassing. I laid the pool stick on the table and attempted to walk away to sit on the sofa to finish my glass of wine.

Reggie apparently had other plans. He grabbed my hand to pull me to him. He bent to kiss me and held my face in his hands as he did so. It was an endearing kiss. Very romantic. It felt different. There was a sincerity in this kiss that I hadn't felt before. I looked up at him because I knew what was coming next. I hoped for what was coming next.

He led me to a bedroom and undressed. I sat on the bed watching him. It was a sight. No words spoken, just intense glances. This felt so different. He took my shoes off, my socks followed. Then he unbuttoned my jeans.

I grabbed his hand to pull him to me for a kiss. It was deep and sensual. Reggie then took off my hoodie and pushed me lightly onto the bed. He grabbed my pants and pulled them from my waist. I kicked them off while he watched.

I then realized that the lights were still on. *Were we really about to get down to business with the lights on?* Yes, because this time was different. This entire set up was different. It was intentional. Reggie flipped me over, slid his arm under my waist and lifted me up onto my knees. My ass was in the air. He rubbed it, slapped it enough to watch it jiggle, but not so hard as to cause pain. I looked back, biting my lip. I liked to watch him please me. That would be hard to do if he were behind me.

Apparently that single motion of me looking back at him with my bottom lip between my teeth, did something to him. In an instant, he pulled me to him and with one hand on my shoulder, he entered me from behind.

I let out a loud sigh and he a loud moan. It was definitely different. We didn't move for about fifteen seconds. It was as if we were calibrating to each other in this position we hadn't been in before. He filled me up and decided to just rest there for a moment. I broke the stillness by backing into him.

"Uhmp" he sounded and it began. Pure. Erotic. Sheer delight is how I would describe it. There was hard thrusting, loud panting, grunting, moaning and hair pulling. It was nasty. Reggie spoke for the first time during sex. Typically our encounters only consisted of moaning and grunting and heavy breathing, but this time there were a lot of "shit" and "damn" flying about. Pounding and ass slapping. In and out, grabbing breasts and more shits and damns.

This was fucking, not love making. I lowered and buried my face in the pillow to muffle my moans. That single motion provided the ability for deeper penetration.

"Shit." Moan, grunt, "Damn". Moan, grunt.

There would be no climax for me, but there was an explosion for Reggie, all over my backside. He cleaned me up and I retreated to the bathroom. If I'm honest, I felt some kind of way. The romance of the way this evening started dissipated to a raunchy fuck session.

I liked Reggie a lot and I typically enjoyed being with him sexually, but this was indeed different. It felt good, but it was not what I was accustomed to with him. It certainly wasn't what I had built up in my mind. There was limited foreplay and I couldn't look at him. I enjoyed watching him please me. To see the pleasure on his face was a part of the experience for me.

After such bonding before, I expected that closeness to continue. Instead, I felt cheap. The night was cheapened. I exited the bathroom with my clothes on, surprised to see Reggie fully dressed as well and putting on his shoes.

He rose and looked down to me and kissed me on the forehead and said, "We have to go."

WHAT??!! I was completely stunned. His presentation affirmed my insecurity. My mouth flew open, but no words came out. I put my shoes on and Reggie reached out his hand for me to take. I did, still pretty shocked.

We walked to the living room and he kissed me and said, "As always, that was great."

My feelings were hurt, I felt cheap. I responded, "So you're done with me now, I guess I should go on home".

Reggie's face changed. I saw what looked to be anger mixed with disappointment. All he said was, "Really, Tab?" He looked at me as if he was waiting for me to respond. I didn't.

He opened his mouth to say something, but shook his head. He drew his lips into his mouth, rubbed his goatee while looking up to the ceiling. He was thinking. Maybe he was considering the right words to say that would explain why the night went the way it did. There were no words. Reggie stood before me, closed his eyes and just let out a quick sigh.

Now I'm confused. I had no words either. I wanted to get an understanding, to clear up any miscommunication that I may have instigated, but there would be no clarification. I didn't know how to express what I felt. I didn't know what to say or ask to make this situation better. We just left the cabin in silence.

He walked me to my car, opened my door for me to get in and quickly shut it when he saw that I was clear and he walked away to his car. Something needed to be said. This was not the way we needed to end the night. But I felt stuck. Unable to articulate my thoughts and feelings. He pulled up onto the gravel drive, waited for me to start my car to follow him. I did, but at the end of the drive, we turned separate ways. I didn't understand why he got so upset when I was the one who felt used. Reggie would explain it to me months later.

Chaz and I reluctantly attended an annual music festival that she was given tickets to. It's hard to pass up free stuff, but neither of us were really feeling it. Chaz spotted Reggie first and asked if he and I were cool.

I lied, "Yeah, we're good."

The truth of the matter is, we were ice cold. No contact whatsoever in about six months. I picked up the phone and dialed most of his number many times, but could not complete the call. I was still lost for words just as I was the last time we saw each other.

Chaz said, "Don't look, but Reggie is literally standing a few yards away to your right."

Excitedly, I immediately looked to my right and we locked eyes. It was like our first sighting.

"Damn, Tab," Chaz grumbled. "I said don't damn look."

I couldn't help myself. Hearing his name made me feel some type of way and to know that he was so close to me made my stomach turn flips. In true Reggie fashion, he was well dressed in distressed jeans, a green and black plaid shirt and gray, green and black Air Max 95's. Reggie came over, exchanged pleasantries with Chaz and looked me square in the eyes. It was awkward at first. It then became extremely awkward when Chaz left to go talk with someone else. So there we stood, face to face after months. The silence was heavy. I kept diverting my eyes only to return to his constant gaze.

Reggie broke the silence with a compliment, "You look good, Tab ... real good."

"Thank you," I replied.

"I've missed you," he said.

I smiled a half smile, I didn't know what to say. The butterflies in my stomach are distracting me. I managed to stutter, "H-how have you been?"

I didn't know how to really respond to his admission to missing me. The truth was that I missed him too and all the feelings that I had for him came rushing back, but I felt the need to protect myself.

"I've been good, I live in Oklahoma now. Moved a couple of months ago. I'm still adjusting to the transition." Reggie looked away, put his hands in his pockets and addressed the awkwardness between us. He obviously felt it too. He shifted his weight from one foot to the other before beginning,"You know, I liked you a lot, Tab and it was jacked up how things ended with us. I thought I was cool until I saw you out here tonight."

Wow. My mouth dropped as he continued.

"All the feelings I had came rushing back. I never told you how I felt. I didn't get a chance to. I guess I should say that I didn't *take* the chance to". He diverted his eyes and drew his lips in. A gesture that I found cute. "It really hurt my feelings that after our last encounter you assumed that I was only spending time with you for sex." Reggie continued, "That assumption seemed to void the effort that I put in to genuinely get to know you, to learn you. Tab, you were much more than sex and your response made me question if all I was to *you* was sex." Reggie tilted his head and looked me in the eyes, "I wanted to call you so many times. I-I just didn't know what to say. Then after a while, I felt like too much time had passed, so I never did."

"Damn. I'm so sorry for the misunderstanding and the lack of communication." I felt flustered. The thoughts in my mind running a mile a minute. I had considered many times what I would say if the opportunity ever presented itself. "That night, I spoke from a place of disappointment and fear, I realized that over time. I wanted to call you too, even dialed your number, but I didn't know how to start the conversation with you. I played a conversation over and over in my mind, but without knowing your position, I was afraid to follow through."

Reggie looked intently. He opened his mouth a couple of times to speak, but I held my hand up so that I could continue. If I didn't get it all out right then, I didn't know when I would have another chance, so I continued, "I later realized that I had expectations that I did not verbalize and when things went south, in my opinion, I didn't have the courage to speak up to clear things up. At that time, I didn't know how to express what I was feeling that night." I let out a sigh of relief. I had held on to all of that for months. Talking with Chaz and my cousins had helped me process things over the last few months.

"Damn, man! I really wish we could have just talked. That's on me too, Tab." Reggie shifted his weight to his left leg. He seemed uncomfortable, almost unsettled. His hands still in his pockets. "I fucked things all up, huh?"

I didn't know if that was a rhetorical question or not, but it was not how I felt. I actually felt that I fucked things up.

"Can I hug you?" He asked innocently.

We hugged it out and played catch up the rest of the night. I was single and so was he, but we were now living in two different states, neither willing to offer accommodations to try. Both likely afraid to do so.

When it was time to go, we said our goodbyes, hugged again and walked away in different directions. And for some reason, that hurt just as much as driving in different directions did months ago. I walked to where Chaz was. She was enjoying a funnel cake at a nearby table. Chaz looked at me with a sincere gaze, offered me some of her dessert and didn't ask any questions. She was with me when I first met Reggie and with me that night. She saw something though. She had to because she hugged me tight and told me things would be ok.

Here lies another lesson that I realized many years later. One that I still struggle with today. If I can give any advice from this situation, it would be *Speak your truth sis! You may never get the opportunity again.* When I finally got home that night, I cried myself to sleep while the

Mary J. Blige *My Life* CD played on repeat all night long. For many years, this album has been the soundtrack to the saddest moments in my life. A few lessons learned in therapy have helped me use this relationship as an example of how unstated expectations often lead to disappointment and how being a little more vulnerable can offer a much different outcome.

Lesson 10: Alex

I took French in college. I wanted a break from Spanish, not many good memories. In addition to needing to fulfill the foreign language requirement, I thought French was a sexy language. I wanted a "Je t'aime" shirt like the one Nia Long wore in *Love Jones*. So when I entered the French class in the first semester of my Junior year of college, I was a little surprised to see so many Black faces. It shocked me even more to notice that there were just as many Black men as there were Black women. Maybe they all thought like me, that French is the sexiest language of all languages. I smiled to myself and thought, *Bonjour, les noirs*. That was really all the French I knew at that time, so I was excited to learn more.

The instructor explained that the first half of the semester would focus more on conversational French. She handed out the syllabi and continued by explaining that we each will be paired with partners this semester with the goal of ultimately being able to have a "decent" conversation with them by semester's end. We were going to be tested on being able to also understand the French language. I thought that I was in over my head and failing wasn't so sexy.

I considered dropping to take up sign language instead or maybe back to Spanish. At least I had two years of high school Spanish to start me off. I looked around the room and noticed that everyone in the class was attentive, no one looked as if they were freaking out. I was all in my head. Madame Bisset returned to the front of the room and asked for us students to introduce ourselves and share one reason we chose French. There were a total of 20 in this class and I listened intently so as to gauge who I wanted as my partner. Out of the 20 people in the class, only five had taken French previously. All of us agreed that French is a sexy, romantic, and intriguing language. After hearing nearly the entire class say that, I wasn't so embarrassed to admit the same. I also shared that my favorite phrase is "Je t'aime." Some in the class knew what that meant and others were not shy about stating that they did not. I recall a classmate, Alex, enlightening the class on what my favorite phrase meant, all while looking me square in the eyes. Now, I don't want to come across as egotistical, but I wondered if this Alex was flirting with me? I gave a sly smirk so as not to appear rude. I was happy to hear Madame Bisset continue with the facilitation of the ice breaker. This allowed the awkward moment between me and Alex to simmer.

I made it through the first full week of the semester. That was no easy feat and time management was a must for sure juggling 15 hours. I learned to be disciplined long ago, but I also wanted to have fun. They say you learn so much about yourself in your college years. I planned on working on that education too. The Education of Tabitha. I showed up to French on a Tuesday morning a little before class started. I liked to get to class early so that I could watch the others walk in. Some people looked extremely sleepy, some looked like they put absolutely no effort into their appearance, and others looked as if they came straight to class from whatever party they attended the night before. I people watched and made up stories about their night before. It was a fun game that I started in high school to pass the time. That day Madame Bisset announced the partnerships, so I wasn't alone people watching. Several more classmates showed up a little early ready to partner up. Madame Bisset arrived right at 9 o'clock and greeted the room, "Bonjour, Bonjour. Permet de s'installer." *What the hell*, I thought and noticed that I was not the only one with a perplexed look. We asked in near unison, "Bonjour", likely because we didn't know what the hell else she said. She must have noticed our looks and the questioning "good morning" because she chuckled. "I said let's get settled". She continued to explain that she did not have the expectation that we would understand all of the things she says in French; however, she would continue to speak the language periodically.

"Conversational foreign languages are best learned while conversing. Pick up clues with what's around you, tone of voice, and body language." The lesson for the day had started and none of us had a clue. Madame Bisset continued, "The more you hear the language, the more you will learn how to emphasize and accentuate certain letters." Her instruction was effortless. She had made her selections and told us that she wanted us to partner up for the remainder of the class. I was partnered with Alex. I was both scared and excited because Alex obviously knew some French and appeared comfortable speaking the language. Making it through a conversation would prove to be a little easier, or so I thought.

"We will begin with our conversation demonstrations next week, so class you're gonna have to get creative with how you and your partner meet to practice and get this done. Don't be averse to meeting after class or over the weekend.", Madame Bisset instructed us. "Since the goal is to have a legitimate conversation, I suggest you be open to meeting in settings that would be conducive to achieving such. Maybe a coffee shop, a bookstore, or the student union."

Those were great ideas, but I volunteered daily after my classes and I became concerned about how Alex and I would meet up to converse.

"I suggest you use the remainder of this class to sync schedules and get to know each other a tad more. "Allons travailler et bonne chance."

Alex chuckled and replied, "Here we go" then turned to me, "I'm Alex, I'm a Scorpio, I'm an only child and I like weed."

A burst of laughter escaped me as that introduction was very unexpected, but I played along. "Nice to meet you Alex, I'm Tabitha. I'm a Pisces, also an only child and I love music."

We performed the customary French greeting of air kisses to each cheek. We laughed a bit more and discussed the best days, times and locations to meet. We decided to "converse" in front of the class about our dream vacation in Nice and the French Riviera. We agreed to meet at Alex's place on Thursday and then again at my place on Saturday. That way if we weren't ready at the conclusion of Saturday's meeting, we could meet on Sunday and/or Monday to polish the presentation. Everyone was expected to present for 10-15 minutes on Tuesday. Chatting with Alex for the remainder of the class was nice, I felt comfortable and felt confident that we could knock this assignment out of the park. We divided the research for Nice and the French Riviera, general information about France and the costs to vacation there. By the time we confirmed that we each had an understanding and the next meeting for Thursday at Alex's place at 8:00 pm, class was over.

I breezed through the rest of the day. Wednesday was a blur. Before I knew it, it was Thursday, "meeting day" with Alex. I had only done about 1/3 of my research and did not want to go there unprepared. I decided skip my last class and volunteering so that I could get my shit together. I decided to leave campus to go to the city library downtown as that was where I was most comfortable and familiar. I did not think this decision through. I didn't consider that not only was the library a nice walk from the downtown parking garage, but it was still hot as hell in September. I was able to gather all of my research and still make it home to shower before heading to Alex's house. No way was I going to go over there smelling like I'd been panhandling on the side of the interstate for hours. The Southern heat was no joke. Typically, I would shower and put on my good smelling lotion when going back out. I hesitated because I was just meeting a classmate. Then I thought, *Tabitha, why not continue your routine,* so I moisturized. I smelled like Bath and Body Works infamous Pearberry. I hopped in my car and put Alex's address in the GPS. I arrived 20 minutes later, approached the door and immediately smelled Alex's marijuana.

I knocked and heard a yell to "Come on in." I did and immediately notice incense burning and candles lit everywhere. They were doing nothing to drown out the overpowering smell of ganja. The lights were dim and it was hazy. Alex emerged from the kitchen and smiled asking, "You can smell it, can't you?" I nodded and we both laughed. I walked over to the dining table and took my notebook from my backpack. I was offered a beverage, my choice between adult or toddler: a wine cooler or a juice box.

Laughing, I asked, "Nothing in between, huh."

Alex replied, "Well there's water ... or milk, but that's no fun."

I turned my nose up at milk and opted for the wine cooler, "So are we about to have fun or work?" Opening my notebook and flipping through to the notes I took at the library, I returned my gaze to Alex.

"Can they not be one and the same? Music or TV?" Alex asked.

"My choice will always be music."

Alex flipped through a mound of CDs and handed me a Bartles and Jaymes Fuzzy Navel. My favorite, anything peach. I had five CDs to choose from: *The Miseducation of Lauryn Hill; Baduizm; Brown Sugar; Share My World;* and *Maxwell's Urban Hang Suite.* I had a hard time choosing one, so I picked two and handed them both to Alex for a final decision.

I opened my wine cooler and looked around through the haze, "This is a nice, cozy little cottage. I especially love the exposed brick and earth tones on the walls."

There weren't many decorations, but I didn't really expect much. Alex didn't seem the type for frills and decor. My thoughts and observations were interrupted by the playing of the "Rimshot Intro".

Alex started talking from the kitchen about the research. I heard about every third word between Erykah and dishes. I said nothing and enjoyed how Alex seemed so involved in the assignment. I typically despised group or partnered assignments because I would end up doing the bulk of the work, but that wasn't seem the case this time. Alex returned to the table with fresh fruit, another Fuzzy Navel, and an ashtray with an incense stick stuck in it.

We spent about an hour working on the project. We sifted through all of the research we both gathered, which was great because that would allow us to spend the rest of the meeting times figuring out how to share our knowledge in French.

Alex told me about old French CDs similar to *Hooked on Phonics,* but for French. I wrote down the suggestion and noticed that I had a nice little buzz. I looked at the empty Fuzzy Navel and margarita bottles. We literally drank a four pack each. I giggled at how in the span of an hour, I managed to drink four Fuzzy Navel wine coolers. My rule of two was out the window. At least our work was done.

There was a knock at the door and I immediately got nervous. *Who could that be?* My mind quickly imagined a gaggle of dudes coming to see the hottie study buddy, me. I was relieved that it was just the Domino's Pizza guy. Alex sat the pizza on the coffee table and went to the kitchen for plates, napkins, and more to drink, "I thought you may be hungry. We have been working for over an hour. Stay for dinner?"

I agreed and walked over to the sofa. We ate and talked, got to know each other a bit more. Alex was a military brat which explains the travel experiences. After about two slices and two juice boxes, because we drank all of the adult beverages, Alex broke the silence. "You are so pretty."

My face warmed, "Thanks. You're not bad on the eyes either." I found it hard make eye contact. I felt a tingle in my stomach and became very mindful of myself. I shifted in my seat and smoothed out my clothes. I was nervous. Instead of looking at Alex's eyes, I focused on other features. Lips. Hands. Anything but eyes. Feeling shy, I was unsure of what to do with my hands. The tingles in my stomach felt like butterflies. Nerves.

Alex touched my cheek, "I like your dimples."

Another shy "Thank you."

I don't know why I was bashful all of a sudden. I had been here for well over two hours at this point. I was the focus and not the French Rivera and this fact made me hyperaware of myself. Typically alcohol lowered my inhibitions and the shyness was nonexistent, but this night was different. I shifted and fiddled with my hands. I couldn't find words.

I looked up and our eyes met. Alex leaned in and kissed me. A peck with a retreat to look in my eyes again as if to check for a response. Leaning in for another peck, I was shocked by my own response. The second peck turned into our mouths slowly opening, with light flicks our tongues touched, and another peck. This time there was no retreat.

Alex cupped by face and kissed me deeper. I kissed back. I enjoyed this. Alex was a good kisser. There was an audible moan and I couldn't tell who it came from.

A hand touched between my legs. I didn't put a stop to the touching because curiosity had taken over. Instead, I moved my hips into Alex's hand as if to give permission to continue the exploration. The kissing resumed, intense. Alex moved from my mouth to my neck. Hands on my breasts, I didn't know what to do with mine. My shirt was pulled over my head revealing my red lace bra.

I bit my bottom lip and wondered what to do next. As if to read my mind, Alex reached behind me with one hand to unhooked my bra while lightly pinching my nipples with the other hand; back and forth between them. I unfastened my pants to see what reaction that would induce and giving me something to do with my hands. My bra hung on one shoulder, one of my breasts exposed, Alex pinched my nipple with more pressure than before while resuming the kisses.

I felt a slight push back as if to signal that I should lie down. I submitted to the subtle physical suggestion. Alex pulled at my jeans to take them off and smiled at my matching red lace panties.

Oh my. Am I really about to do this?

My heart was beating fast because I knew what was about to happen, but at the same time I had no clue what it would be like. This was a serious first.

Alex rubbed my legs, both at the same time, moving from my ankles all the way up to my center. My lady parts throbbed and I closed my eyes to brace for what I thought was coming. The anticipation was strong. There was a tug at my panties, so I lifted my backside to allow Alex to take them off. My eyes were closed. My mind was back on what to do with my hands. I was still, concentrating on being relaxed as much as I could. My legs were pushed open and I felt fingers touch my wetness—it felt so good.

Ok, I like that, I thought.

I opened one eye for a peek and noticed Alex's fingers glistened with my juices. Another kiss and more throbbing. Alex sat up and licked my juice from those glistening fingers. A moan escaped my lips. That simple motion turned me on more. I wanted Alex to lick my center and not finger me. As if to read my mind, Alex lowered between my legs and dined on my sweet spot as if that pizza was not enough. It was a feeling like no other.

The sensation of fingers reinserted inside me while Alex's tongue flicked on my clitoris was almost an unbearable pleasure. Such an intense feeling, I climaxed faster than I ever had before. Alex moaned softly and didn't stop, as if to not waste a single drop. I lifted my butt slightly only to feel a wetness trace from my honey pot to my anus. A second wave took over. It was as if that was anticipated. My eyes closed. My body jerked erratically. My moans loud. There was a lot of wetness. Alex moved up to suckle on my breasts, one at a time, back and forth.

There was a pause. I opened my eyes to see Alex above me, smiling with delight as if a major goal had been accomplished. I didn't know what was next, but I knew that I felt good. I didn't rush to grab up my clothes. I continued to lie there, looking up at Alex.

"Did you like that?"

In all honesty I loved it, but I simply replied, "I did."

"You don't have to do anything in return, I just had the urge to please you and felt confident that I could," Alex admitted.

I smiled and continued looking up at Alex, not breaking the gaze with even a blink. Alex bent to suckle my breasts more, and it felt so good and I felt myself getting aroused all over again. All of those sensations and responses were so new to me. It seemed as if all of the cells in my body were firing with every ounce of energy I had. I just wanted it to last for as long as possible.

I grabbed Alex's head to signal that I was pleased and wanted the kissing and sucking to continue. With attention back down between my legs, I pushed into Alex's hand. We both moaned. Kiss, kiss, long, loud suckling on my breasts, back and forth. I was pulsing once more. With two fingers inside of me pushing on a spot I didn't know existed, Alex caused a feeling I couldn't put into words.

Alex's tongue was back on my clit. A sudden urge to pee caused me to tense up, but Alex whispered for me to "relax, let it go!"

"Let what go?" I asked.

"If you feel like you need to pee, it's not pee. Let that go, you'll like it and thank me later."

Confused about the sensations occurring in my body and not having a clue as to what I was being told to do, I agreed, "I'll try to relax and let it go ..."

"Don't think about it, just do it," Alex said, kissing my stomach before heading back down.

Those two fingers pushed in further and that sensation surged through me. A huge gushing release and I heard Alex moan deep, "There you go. Mhmmmm."

Alex lifted again to look at me as she took her shirt off to expose her own bare breasts. She hovered over me, lining up one breast with my mouth. I took the not so subtle hint and suckled her back. I returned the favor as if I had done this before. Surprisingly, it felt natural. I simply did what I liked and she responded in kind.

She rose slowly to take off her shorts. Alex returned her breast to my mouth. She liked that feeling. She moved her hips into mine and we found a groove, grinding each other as if a slow dance was underway.

She touched herself through her panties and the back of her hand rubbed up against my wetness. I sucked, she moved. She requested that I suck harder. I complied and she moved faster against her own fingers, which in turn caused the back of her hand to rub faster against me. She knew what she was doing.

"Harder," she requested. I obliged.

She removed her breast from my mouth to kiss me deep. She was panting as she continued to grind against me and her own hand. With her free hand, she caressed me lightly. We were pelvis to pelvis. Alex removed her panties and positioned her legs in such a way that both of our clitoris' were receiving the most erotic of touches and before I knew it, Alex climaxed softly on top of me. She slid down to my side to lie on the couch, kissed my cheek as she did so.

She admitted, "I hadn't had an orgasm in over a year. I'm glad you helped me do that."

I smiled and said, "Sure."

There was a slight awkwardness for me as we lay next to each other. I retreated to my head wondering, *what's next?* I wondered what the encounter meant. I replayed the moments that led up to my first sexual experience with a woman. It flowed organically. Effortlessly. The moments leading up to the greatest climax I had ever experienced felt no different than being with a man.

As if she sensed my internal dialogue, she whispered in my ear, "This doesn't make you a lesbian." Thinking I was a lesbian was the last thing on my mind, but I did wonder what all of this did mean. She continued, "I don't even identify as a lesbian; not even as bisexual. There are just some women that I am extremely attracted to and occasionally I get the opportunity to explore that attraction. I love men. I love having sex with men. I love everything about a man. I don't feel that way about women ... not even specific types of women. Sometimes I see or meet a woman and there is this strong attraction to just her. It's happened maybe three times in my life. This is my second time with a woman and I totally understand if we never speak of this again."

I appreciated her transparency and her attempt to comfort me. I admired her freedom. She was comfortable in her own truth and took the time to explain it to me. What she said made so much sense because I never considered being with a woman and hadn't ever looked at a woman in a sexual way at all. But I thoroughly enjoyed being with Alex.

She said, "I came to college for a good education and believe that all of that education doesn't have to occur in the classroom."

I like the way she justified this. I may use that, *I received a very comprehensive education in college*. I chuckled aloud. Alex asked what I was laughing at and I shared my thoughts. She laughed too.

Alex and I went on to ace the French conversation. We did so well, Madame Bisset allowed us to remain partners. We also continued to play around. I enjoyed the way we explored with each other. I learned so much about what I like sexually. I learned so much about my own body and how I experience pleasure.

We had an understanding that this was just between us. We would date men and live our individual lives. If one reached out to the other to hook up and we were both in agreement, we made it happen. If the time wasn't right, we'd schedule another time. At times we skipped a class or two.

We even took an out of town trip, posted up in the hotel room and explored all weekend. We watched porn and learned some new things that we liked. Our extracurricular education was mutual, open minded, and our little secret. I liked having a secret and having such taught me the art of privacy. When we decided to stop, sometime in our Senior year, that too was mutual.

I appreciated Alex for her openness and transparency and to this day, I think of her when I shrink and allow the opinions of others to impact me. Thoughts of her remind me to host a solid presentation of who I am. Remembering her reminds me to stand firm in my individuality and resist trying to fit in some box that someone that I don't know, like or respect tries to put me in. Be brave ... that's the lesson Alex taught me and I remain forever grateful for it.

Lesson 11: Kevin

My second engagement was a real engagement. At least it was real to me. I mean, we were grown and there was a ring, engagement photos, and real wedding planning. We picked out invitations, I bought a dress, and had singers lined up. I had a ring, and it was a ring that I liked. We mailed out invitations and had begun receiving RSVPs. A DJ was hired, a caterer reserved, and a cake tasting. I had a really nice ring. It doesn't get any more real than all of that.

Well, what's real for one person isn't necessarily real for the next. Whenever I had doubts about my intended's level of commitment, I would play with my ring. I relied on it to prove to me that things were real. We had plans to have a private ceremony and honeymoon in the Caribbean. We had such big plans.

I met Kevin through a friend. That seemed to be my M.O. for a few years, meeting guys via set-ups or coincidental meetings while out with friends. He was attractive, I especially liked his bald head. He had a Tyrese type vibe.

We met on a blind double date. We had not spoken prior and we each received only physical descriptions of the other, no pictures. I was totally out of my comfort zone and I was hella nervous. I almost backed out. I called two of my cousins and one of my friends in hopes that they would talk me out of going, but I was encouraged by them all to go and enjoy myself. *Shit!*

I sat at the foot of my bed for an hour attempting to concoct the perfect excuse for backing out at the last minute. I was so committed to finding an out, that I didn't have adequate time to put together a good outfit. My chosen outfit showed my lack of planning and my lackluster attempt to put myself together: white V-neck t-shirt, jeans, and blush pink sandals. I didn't even iron.

We decided to meet up at a local sports bar known for bomb wings and karaoke. I walked into the bar, my group already seated waved for me to join. I noticed immediately that there was only the couple present.

Shit, Shit, Shit!! He flaked.

Seeing the *WTF* look on my face, the only guy in the group said, "Kevin is running a little late, but he's coming."

I rolled my eyes and pulled out a chair to sit. My seat hadn't warmed before our waitress was at the table for my drink order. I ordered a Cosmo, laughing good-naturedly at the white guy on the stage singing *Thong Song* by Sisqo. There were two buckets of wings, loaded fries, and onion rings already on the table. I relaxed a bit and enjoyed the show. He didn't sound too bad.

I kept watching the door, anxious for Kevin to arrive so I could see if all the effort I had exerted was worth it. White Sisqo was replaced on the stage by a group of ladies singing SWV's *Weak*. I was embarrassed for them, but I suppose untalented singers are what make Karaoke fun.

I turned to say something to the couple and glanced at the door. I recognized him immediately. The description I was given was spot on. Our eyes met and he flashed a nice smile. For a moment, I wished I had at least threw my t-shirt in the dryer to knock some of the wrinkles out. Our mutual friend waved him over to the table and as he approached, Kevin looked at me like I was the only person there and introduced himself.

He offered a hand to shake, "Tabitha?"

I nodded and took his hand.

"I'm Kevin."

I was slightly impressed, but still apprehensive, "Hi Kevin."

"My apologies for being late, I didn't anticipate the traffic."

I smiled. Everyone exchanged pleasantries which was followed by Kevin asking if I wanted another drink. The waitress was Janey-on-the-spot, already at the table to take Kevin's drink order. "I'll have a Long Island Iced Tea and let's get this pretty lady another of what she had."

An assertive man, I smiled to myself. Kevin leaned in to ask me a question that I didn't hear because three girls are singing TLC's "Baby, Baby, Baby" just a few feet away from us.

When there was a lower moment in the song, he repeated his question, "Do you sing?"

I replied, "In my shower mostly, rarely in public."

"So you wouldn't do karaoke?" he asked.

"I'd have to be extremely comfortable." I realized in that moment that I was worried about being judged more than anything.

We ordered more wings and fries for the table and I had no intention of eating pretty or being accommodating. I requested all flats with extra sauce on the side. My companions laughed and stated in almost unison, "high maintenance." This comment started a very insightful conversation about passing judgements based upon someone's food order. Things became more lighthearted and I relaxed a bit more.

Maybe it was the second Cosmo, maybe it was the karaoke which I discovered the theme for the night was *"Back in the Day."* A young man was bopping up and down while singing "I Like The Way" by Hi-Five, sounding so much like the lead singer Tony that we all had to look twice. We debated music, TV shows and movies. We ladies laughed, high-fived, and side eyed the men. We enjoyed the karaoke until the show was over.

Kevin walked me to my car and shared how much he enjoyed me and how he didn't want the night to end. I honestly enjoyed my time with him as well and the fact that he wasn't bad on the eyes made me consider hanging with him a little longer. The couple we were with suggested that we head downtown or to a strip club. The guys voted for both. They suggested that we all hop in their Escalade so we could hang out like we were all back in our 20s.

I must admit that I ended up having a fabulous time. Kevin was most definitely a fun loving guy. He was a little handsy, but not in a sex offender type way. That night was my first time at a strip club and I was all in my head. It must have been obvious because Kevin leaned in to whisper in my ear, his lips grazing my lobe, "No one will judge you for having a good time." It was as if he read my mind. I realized that night, in situations like this, I was more comfortable as a spectator.

I received my first lap dance, courtesy of Kevin. I found myself wondering how the young lady moved her ass in such a way and was all in my head about what to do with my hands. I thought about Alex and how free she was. That helped some. It was an interesting experience, but I had never felt more prudish in my life. The night ended around 3am when I was taken back to my car at the sports bar.

Kevin escorted me to my car, " So little lady, can I see you again real soon?"

He opened my car door and I asked, "When did you have in mind?"

He smiled a sly smile and said, "Lunch or dinner," he looked at his watch, "today?"

I was shocked. We had just met and he was wanting even more time with me.

He continued, "I can't say enough how much I enjoyed hanging out with you. I simply want another opportunity to do so, to get to know more about you. I want to hang with just you."

I was flattered and agreed. We exchanged phone numbers and agreed to keep each other updated on our day to figure out the best time to meet up for a bite to eat.

On my drive home, I thought about how much I loved when men showed interest the way Kevin did. He took initiative. Expressed his interest. A man who said what he wanted, and was direct, complimentary, and respectful. That would be my experience with him for much of our time together.

During lunch the next day, Kevin was more reserved. He seemed nervous, but attentive. I caught him staring at me several times and wondered what his thoughts were. The conversation was light, but informative. The energy was magnetic. I knew I wanted to be in his presence as much as I could. I wanted to learn more and more with each detail I received about who he was. The conversation flowed as if we had known each other much longer than we had.

As weeks passed, we became very familiar with each other, speaking almost daily. Weeks turned in to months and on the year anniversary of our meeting, he asked me to be his "lady."

We took trips, hung out as friends, behaved like lovers. I felt extremely comfortable with Kevin. The relationship we had was refreshing. It had been a long while since I'd felt this way. That year went by so quickly.

On the outside we were the perfect couple. Successful in our respective careers. Traveling and enjoying life. He took care of me following a surgery and did a damn good job. I had fallen hard for him. By a year and a half, we had moved in together. This was the first time that I had shared living space with a man. I was on foreign ground, but felt committed to making it work.

This day-to-day closeness revealed the cracks in our relationship. We didn't speak nearly as much as we had when living apart. He often fell asleep on the couch and the sex we had was dwindling fast. The norm for us had been physical intimacy almost daily, but the act of physical touch and sex become more of something we did just to say we were doing it.

He cooked, I cleaned. We took care of bills and handled business. A business is what this relationship had become. I began to feel as if I were losing him. How could we be drifting apart so soon after moving in together. There were times when we would sit at the table having a quiet dinner together, struggling to find words to speak. Once we got past the "How was your day? What did you have for lunch?" questions, we were lost for words. A stark contrast to our dinners before being so full of updates about our day or plans we wanted to make. It was such an uncomfortable time. It seemed the more I inquired about what was going on in our relationship, the more he denied any problems, the more I felt a sinking feeling in my gut. The disconnect was mounting.

Six months after moving in together, just a couple weeks shy of our two year anniversary, Kevin proposed with an amazing ring during a dinner prepared at our apartment by a private chef.

This is what the distance was these last few months, he was gearing up to ask me to marry him, I thought before agreeing to be his wife. He kissed me softly and hugged me tight. I felt butterflies in my stomach. Flutters of magnetism to the man I longed for. The physical closeness that I had missed was evident in my desire to hold onto him longer, tighter.

"You ok, babe?"

"I am. Just overjoyed." I looked over Kevin's shoulder at my ring. I was engaged.

The euphoria of being newly engaged lasted about a month and then we were back to being distant strangers living under one roof. It was like we were living parallel lives.

On the outside, we were relationship goals. On the inside, things were more shallow than I had realized. The foundation was shaky and unstable.

It seems that just on the other side of year two into our relationship, all hell broke loose. While I had a beautiful pear shaped 1.75 karat diamond engagement ring and wedding invitation samples sitting on the dining table, Kevin was gallivanting around town as if he were single.

I learned one evening while preparing dinner, that he had engaged in three separate relationships with other women over the course of our entire relationship. I answered his phone that evening and hearing the voice of a woman named Belinda produced a sinking feeling in my stomach that I hadn't felt before.

She knew who I was, but she was brand new to me. She had no problems telling me about she and Kevin's relationship. She told me that she learned about me via social media when Kevin's sister made a congratulatory post for our engagement. I was encouraged to "check his social media" while I had his phone. She said there I would find messages with two other women, Karen and Alisha, speaking about meeting up and rehashing past visits. My heart sunk. Belinda shared that she attempted to contact me via social media, but I hadn't responded. She said that she was calling Kevin this evening to tell him about the messages she had sent to me.

As I was learning all the things my new fiancé had been up to for months, I began to question everything I thought I knew about Kevin and the relationship I thought I had. Things began to make sense. The times he would be M.I.A. for hours. The sleeping on the couch. The lack of sex. *How could I have been so foolish?*

I was the only one not receiving the affections and attention I longed for. Kevin had fucking options. I was furious. I was devastated. Kevin entered the kitchen as I was moving from his social media to his text messages. I gasped and clutched my proverbial pearls at the sight of breasts that did not belong to me. A knife still in my hand and dinner long forgotten, I saw clips of videos of one of the women masturbating. Requests for dick pics and for him to be inside of them "again." *Again?!*

I raised my eyes as a single tear fell, heart pounding. Stomach going crazy. "Shit", Kevin muttered. Before I knew it, I threw his phone at his face. I missed, but clipped his ear. I couldn't speak. No sound was available to me. I quietly cried as I moved past Kevin to retrieve my bag and keys. I left. Knife still in hand.

I returned the next day when I thought he was at work, packed up all that I could and went to stay with Chaz for a few days. I was embarrassed. *How could I had not seen this?*

I cried myself to sleep for four nights straight, ignoring Kevin's calls and text messages. There was no explaining his way out of this. He began calling my friends looking for me. When he called Chaz, I had her tell him the engagement was off and that I would have the remaining items picked up soon.

Chaz and I stayed up many nights planning Kevin's demise. We came up with the wildest ideas before we reminded each other that we had actual careers and reputations to uphold. We weren't in college anymore and could no longer blame criminal acts on youth and naiveté.

I quickly found my own apartment and moved in from Chaz's place. It was quiet. It was lonely. I had too much time and space to think and overthink. I continued to ignore calls from Kevin. I needed no explanation. I had no intention to allow myself to be willfully lied to. With each call and subsequent voicemail, my heart ached.

My first month in my apartment was brutal. Chaz was afraid to leave me alone some nights. Thank goodness she didn't. I couldn't face my other friends and family just yet, so I hid out in that apartment for 31 days straight. I went to work and to the grocery store, and that was it. As I came to terms that there would be no wedding, no more Tab and Kev, I realized that I was extremely disappointed and still very sad, but I continued to operate without outwardly proving that my personal life was in shambles.

One day, I was sitting in the floor of my apartment listening to Whitney Houston's greatest hits reminding myself that for the entire relationship, I had been sharing the man I planned to marry. I laughed. I laughed hysterically as "Saving All My Love for You" began to play. Listening to those words, the laughter turned to tears. I began to cry uncontrollably. I replayed every inch of our relationship asking, *How could I have missed that?* Kevin was damn good because I was not suspicious one bit. I looked inward regarding the distance that was occurring between us. *What had I done to push him away? What could I have done to improve our station?*

I stopped Whitney and decided to play the playlist I created for moments such as this. "Alexa, shuffle my playlist *Heartbreak Hotel.*" My process was to let it all out. To feel all the pain at once so that the next day, I could get back to living. Toni Braxton's, "Un-Break My Heart" began to play. I pressed rewind, going back to memories of the first day that we met. I thought of the day he asked me to move in with him. The day that he proposed was forever etched in my mind. I remembered the tinge of discomfort in my stomach at times, the feelings I mistook for indigestion.

I realized that those were feelings that showed up periodically throughout our relationship. There would be an interaction or things that he would say that produced those uncomfortable feelings. *You dummy, that was your intuition trying to clue you in that something was wrong.* I never explored the feelings. I hadn't questioned the root cause of them or examined the instances in which they occurred. I had ignored it.

Three additional women in two years. I began to wonder about them. Wanted to know what they had that I didn't. Wanted to know what they did that I didn't do. Wondered what was wrong with me.

I screamed. I cried hysterically. I was out of control, throwing a full fledge temper tantrum in my living room, but not because my fiancé cheated and now we have broken up. I was losing it because I was blaming myself for his shitty behavior and bad choices and I didn't know how to stop it. My mind was moving at the speed of light, replaying every sexual experience, every date, every trip. I picked apart my actions and reactions. I questioned if I were enough.

The more I tore myself apart, the more upset I became. I had a panic attack. I couldn't catch my breath. My heart was racing. *Is this what a broken heart feels like?* I struggled to catch my breath. I felt like

I was going to die. I knew I needed to calm down, but I was struggling with shallow breathing and destructive thoughts. With my head tilted back, my eyes wide, I tried to breathe. *Breathe Tabitha, breathe!*

My soul began to speak. Nicer words came. Encouraging words came to me. *Tab, you aren't dying. You are stronger than you're giving yourself credit for right now. Breathe babygirl. Breathe.*

I wiped my eyes and took deep breaths. *That's it, sweet girl. Breathe.* My soul was maternal. I supposed it was exactly what I needed in that moment. A comfort that sounded wise and nurturing. It helped tremendously.

The song switched to Faith Evans's rendition of "Love Don't Live Here Anymore". The encouragement continued, *It's better that you find out now than to marry him and found out later. Breathe in deep. He doesn't deserve you. You are so worthy of better. Exhale slowly.* The tears continued to fall, but I had calmed a bit. The encouraging voice sounded like me, but wiser, calmer, and more comforting.

I laid on the floor and listened to the song. When it ended, I asked Alexa to play Rose Royce's version. I sang along, "You abandoned me, love don't live here anymore. Just a vacancy, love don't live here anymore."

My sad love songs continued to play as I sang and danced around the house. My pity party was slowly ending and the sad songs began to empower me. It was like kindred spirits aligning to heal deep wounds caused by people we trusted. People who shouldn't have cause such pain.

It took quite a bit of time to get over my break up with Kevin. I have very fond memories that bring about tearful moments and crying spells, but I don't beat myself up nearly as much for not seeing the signs of his infidelity. I no longer blame myself and take responsibility for his actions. The embarrassment of a failed engagement kept me away from friends and family for some time. I hadn't wanted to face questions that I wasn't sure how to answer.

The lesson here is a tough one: I need to listen to my intuition. I realize now that I was so wrapped up in the activities we shared, the traveling, going out to play pool, game night parties at the house and even the quiet moments. We had a lot of fun. It wasn't all bad. Then after he proposed, my focus became the wedding. I became obsessed with the planning. Not the marriage, but the wedding. *But what happens after the wedding?* When I took away the fun, there was so much I didn't know. I was only getting a fraction of him and when my intuition would rise, I would subconsciously protect myself. It's hard to connect when one is protecting themselves and the other is half present in the relationship. It was doomed to fail continuing in that manner.

Lesson 12: Therapy

It's a beautiful day. The sun is out and is warming up the world. Days like this I wish I was outside instead of the office. I have been so distracted at work thinking about this beautiful day and my upcoming therapy session. I surprisingly have no anxiety about the fact that I don't know what to expect. I know that we will review my reflections from journal entries, but I don't know where the session will take me, and I'm ok with that. I haven't felt the desire to prepare for my session in an attempt to be ready for whatever Dr. Drea pulls out of me. There is no longer a desire for her to pull. I want to freely share and receive a perspective different from my own.

In my car, I open the sunroof and let the windows down and turn my music on shuffle. The song that plays first is so fitting. Tamia's *Can't Get Enough* has always made me feel happy. Giddy, I imagine such a love. This song always puts me in a good mood and makes me wanna dance. I arrive to Dr. Drea's office a little bit early with the plan to scroll social media while I sit in the waiting, but her door is already open.

"Come on in, Tabitha," Dr. Drea shouts from the inside of her office. I enter and there is a bottled water sitting on the table next to my normal spot on the loveseat. She enters the room with a mug of tea, "How's it going? You look good."

I jump right in, "I'm doing very well today, Doc. You know, memory is a funny thing." I open my water and take a sip. "I think most people understand the role that perception plays, but we don't often readily understand how much of a role emotions play. I believe that when we are able to step away from the emotions *and* look at things from a different perspective, that memory changes. It clears up a bit. I also recognize that this is a difficult thing to do, emotions also drive out perspective."

Therapy has become such a staple in my growth process. I look out of the window and follow the beams of light shine through and onto the amethyst crystals on the Kleenex box holder. I watch the fragmented light dance. It makes me smile.

"That's good insight, Tabitha. Continue, please."

I take a deep breath and exhale with more force than intended.

"Well, since our last session, I reviewed the journal entries for Reggie, Alex, and Kevin. I wasn't as emotional as I was at the start of this assignment. By the time I had these experiences, I had a bit more insight. I could see how I had matured. I actually started to include the lessons I was learning in those journal entries. I suppose the biggest take away is that I played a role in how certain situations went down. I also now realize that I hadn't always carried the lessons learned with me."

"Explain further Tabitha. Are you speaking about anything or anyone in particular?"

"Well ... with Reggie. That situation was all me. I fucked that up all by myself," I pause. I look at Dr. Drea to check for her reaction to my admission. Her face still soft and comforting. I feel emotion welling up inside of me, but I can't name it right now. In actuality, no matter the emotion, the physical manifestation of said emotions is always the same. Tears. I look at my hands to keep from making eye contact. The silence that Dr. Drea uses so well settles between us now. An early appearance this time. It's my cue to continue. "Going back to read those journal entries and taking a look back with eyes fresh with growth and maturity, I can see how I allowed insecurity and my silence to sabotage a good thing."

Dr. Drea smiles softly and says, "That's impressive Tabitha. Tell me what made the situation with Reggie so good."

"It seemed to work for us no matter how difficult our schedules. I felt wanted and he made a genuine effort to spend time with me."

"So, was it perfect for that time?"

"I don't know if I would say perfect, but it worked for that time. We never discussed feelings for each other when we were in the thick of it. Those admissions came much later, after I had messed things up."

"You've mentioned that a couple of times, you messing things up. How did you do that, Tabitha?"

"Whew." My eyes burn with tears trying to escape. "I assumed that he was using me for sex and rather than ask about my status with him, or offering him the opportunity to make it clear to me, I operated from that frame of mind. That assumption. Things with him ended abruptly. No conversation about the misunderstanding, just nothing." I allow my mind to try to remember Reggie. Details long since gone from my mind. I remember the feelings though. "I saw him six months or so later and found out that he had real feelings for me. He shared how my assumption back then made him feel, but by that time we had settled into different lives."

"Mhm. So, what kept you two from expressing how you felt?"

"I can't say for him, but for me, I would say a mix of fear and the lack of self-awareness at that time. I have come to realize that there were several moments in my life where I just floated with no intentions, no goals, nothing. Just living day to day." I took a deep breath to grasp what I just admitted. "Honestly Dr. Drea, I don't know how I made it this long without any significant trauma. I was so careless with my life … with my body, my mind," and there are the tears I had fought so hard to hold back. I couldn't connect them with sadness though. Maybe empathy.

Dr. Drea leans in, "What are you feeling, Tabitha?"

"A mix of emotions." I take a moment to collect my thoughts. "I just realized in this moment that I must have been divinely protected throughout my teen and young adult years because I escaped, with some hurt feelings and a few errors, but for the most part unscathed. On the other hand, I feel stupid." *Shit!* "Like I missed out on important life lessons and had to learn as best I could through trial and error. Like, I feel that I should know so much more about love and how to navigate relationships."

Dr. Drea looks perplexed, "If not by experience Tabitha, how else do you expect to learn certain things? No one can teach you how to love or how to be a partner. They can share their experiences and what works for them, but ultimately, how you execute that is up to you. For instance, I can help to teach you how to love me, but whether you do and what you do is still your choice. As far as relationships, it's not a one size fits all. It's all customized based on the individual we are in relationship with."

I nod because that makes a lot of sense. "I get that Dr. Drea. I suppose my questions are, how does one come to value their body rather than giving it away freely? How does one begin to communicate effectively and without fear of rejection? Are those lessons that come with practice?"

"In some respects, yes. I can tell you that you are valuable and why, but Tabitha *you* have to see and feel that in order to move as such. I can teach you principles of effective communication and generally speaking, they will work, but when you come across someone who isn't a good communicator, you have to learn how to pivot." Dr. Drea breaks it all the way down for me.

"See that's the thing, I didn't get any preliminary lessons. I'm just winging it and have failed miserably."

"We are all 'just winging it,' Tabitha. Let me preface what I am about to say with this: I say this in love and in no way intend to offend."

"Oh shit!"

Dr. Drea smirks, "I would argue that you did receive those preliminary lessons, you just didn't apply them, nor did you pivot when needed." I'm sure my face has a dumb look on it because Dr. Drea continues, "You played sports, right?"

I nod.

"You had to learn to communicate with your teammates verbally and nonverbally. As an only child, it's reasonable to assume that you had some type of relationship with one or both of your parents."

"Yes, I can see your point."

"So all of that taught you, Tabitha. Even poor lessons are lessons. For example, a man grows up without a father figure. He yearned for a positive male presence in his life and while he and his mother were always close, he wanted that masculine energy. He needed balance. He has his own children and turns out to be an excellent father. Where did he learn that Tabitha?"

"His mother?"

"Maybe some lessons about parenting derived from the teachings of his mother, but to be a father. He applied what he yearned for, what was missing in his life. He provided his children what he imagined he would have received had he had a father in his life. Do you see what I'm saying?"

I nod again. The silence is back. Dr. Drea allows me time to process things. I quickly run all of what she shared through several situations and can see how it all could apply.

"So you mentioned two other people, Alex and Kevin. I have heard you mention Kevin, when you first started therapy with me, but not an Alex. Tell me about him."

I smiled and averted my eyes, "Alex isn't a guy." I peek up at Dr. Drea, searching for a reaction. There isn't one. She has a hell of a poker face. I continue, "I had an eighteen-month fling with a woman in college. It was actually one of the best experiences I've had in my life. Alex was more than the answer to a curiosity that I didn't know I had; she taught me about freedom and to care less about the opinions of others."

"Ok, how did she do that?"

"After our first encounter, she reassured me that I didn't have to label myself as lesbian or bisexual. She was open about herself and how she didn't identify as such either, but occasionally found a particular woman attractive enough to explore. Before her, I never considered being intimate with a woman. I didn't look at a woman as a potential partner or lover, and I still don't. I suppose it started like many other sexual encounters where I abdicated control over my own body and allowed Alex to have her way. Just so happened that I enjoyed it. We both dated men at the same time. I remember wondering where the expectation of publicly identifying your sexual identity to other people originated. Alex helped me understand that it's nobody's business what I do."

"How did that feel?"

"I felt liberated. It initially started out as excitement that I had a secret, but with time I understood the difference between a secret and a personal matter."

"What's the difference you've come to understand?"

"A secret implies that something is occurring that is wrong. A personal matter simply means it's no one's fucking business!"

"Well said, Tabitha. So I noticed a slight reaction when I erroneously assumed that Alex was a man. What was that?"

Hmmm. I didn't think I had a reaction.

Dr. Drea clarified, "You broke eye contact ... seemed almost shy to speak on the matter. What was that?"

Ahhh. I pull my hand to my chin as I consider how to answer this question. Dr. Drea allows me the time. "It's just a situation that I've kept to myself for so long. I've not spoken about it because I didn't want any judgement."

"So is there some shame attached to that?"

Shame. Looking at the amethysts glimmer on that Kleenex box, I deeply consider her question. *Shame?* "I don't know if its shame as much as it is avoiding subjecting myself to other people's opinions of me. Judgement."

There is more silence as I reminisce on how free I felt and how I yearned for that freedom on a regular basis. "Dr. Drea, sometimes I forget that my choices are personal and that it doesn't matter what other people think about them. I need to remember that more." I stare into space a bit longer, looking at the sparkling stones.

"Is that all about Alex?"

"Pretty much. It was a pleasurable, a very pleasurable experience that I still think of fondly."

"Are you still in touch?"

"No. We lost contact about a year before I met Kevin. She got married and started a family. I'm not sure where she is now, but I do think of her sometimes. Mostly about what she taught me."

"Ok. And Kevin, when you went back to read your journal entries about him, did you see anything different?"

I shifted in my seat. Speaking about Kevin is easier now, but the remembered pain was like scratching a healed wound until it bled again. A deep sigh before answering, "I'm impulsive and spoiled. I tend to only see what I want to see so long as it aligns with what I want. I looked back at my experience with Kevin and what I have experienced since then and see that pattern." *Damn! I don't want to cry. Don't cry.* "I can get fixated on things where I feel I have some control to make up for the lack of control in other aspects of my life."

"You see this as a pattern that you have continued in relationships?"

"Yep. I think now I am somewhat better able to adjust when I become aware of it. In my current situation, I find myself asking, '*Tab what are you doing?*' yet I keep doing that questionable thing."

"You mean the situation with the two guys?"

"Yes."

"Ok, so with the insight you have gained from your relationship with Kevin and the realization that you are repeating patterns, what do you do with all of that?"

If I knew, I would do it! "Nothing." I let that sink in a bit. "I don't decide. It's like I would prefer for someone else to make the choice or tell me what to do."

"Why give your power away?"

Whew ... damn Doc. That one stings a bit. "I suppose I didn't view it as me giving my power away as much as me trying not to hurt anyone's feelings. Like, what if I make the wrong choice?" I look at the digital clock behind Dr. Drea and that causes her to look down at her watch. We are out of time.

"Ok, so Tabitha, I want you to sit with that a little bit and we can discuss at your next session. What keeps you from trusting yourself, thus leading to you giving your power away? Also, let's put more thought and consideration into your current situation with these two guys. Use your journaling to process what is happening there."

I nod and gather my things. It's been a while since Dr. Drea has given me homework. "Thanks, Doc. I appreciate you. See you next time."

"Bye Tabitha, be careful."

Lesson 13: Maurice vs.Charles

Growing up, my mom would get up on Saturday mornings to clean. I knew it was time for me to get up to help when I heard Teddy Pendergrass yell about turning off the lights. Saturday mornings were for cleaning, and the music made it a bearable experience. With the same routine and different music selections, my Saturday mornings are similar. Cleaning and listening to the music is when I do my best thinking, planning, and remembering. I can easily slip into a daydream if the right song hits. This morning I'm feeling a little Jill Scott-ish. Mid way through "A Long Walk" and my chores are complete and boy am I tired. I have a list of things to accomplish today and I am determined to get them done, but first I must rest a while. I lie on the couch and allow Jill to sing me into a nap with one of my favorites, "He Loves Me".

I wake to the doorbell ringing and no music. I am a little disoriented because not only did the doorbell startle me, but I had been having the most vivid dream one could have while taking a simple, mid-morning nap. I sit on the edge of my couch attempting to regain my composure. I don't know if I should go shower or check my porch as I am sure the doorbell was alerting me that a package had arrived. "Alexa, shuffle Jill Scott *The Light of the Sun* album," I ask as I remember the dream I just had. Of all songs to play first, "So Gone" starts its sexy intro. I smirk, lie back on the couch, lift my feet to the coffee table and replay my dream.

I'm at a house party, but not at my house. Several people from my job and office building are there. There is plenty of food and the drinks are flowing. There is loud trap music playing. In the corner is Maurice, the strong, quiet dentist from the 7th floor of my office building. He's always pleasant, calls me by name when he speaks. A very polite and seemingly respectful man. He's sexy as hell too. Tall, caramel complexion, bald head, salt and pepper goatee, and perfect teeth. I've honestly been lusting after this man for a while now. I've also checked his left ring finger every Monday, just to make sure he didn't get married over the weekend. We catch eyes. I half smile; he shows all of his teeth. He has to know what that perfect smile does to women. He's entertaining two of the newest attorneys in the building, smiling and nodding, while looking directly at me. Is he flirting with me? I ask myself. I flirt back by flashing my dimples and biting my bottom lip. I had always felt something when close to him, either in an elevator or passing each other at the coffee shop in the office lobby. It's a feeling I can't explain, but has me wanting to explore. I just assumed it was all in my head, but tonight, I'm seeing something more. Maurice is actually flirting with me.

He rises from the chair he was seated and walks toward me. His entire existence excites me. He has on a pair of nice jeans, a simple gray V-neck tee shirt with the sleeves rolled up showing perfect biceps and triceps that appear more pronounced when he lowers his arms. I touch my bottom lip to make sure that I'm not drooling ... I'm not, but he's worthy of such a reaction.

"Hey," he says. He stands a good foot or more taller than me and I can smell his cologne perfectly.

I look up at him and say, "Hello Maurice, how are you?"

He flashes that Colgate smile and replies, "I'm real good now,"

Oh he's flirting, flirting, I think. "It's nice to see you out socially. You look different in casual clothes," he says.

I reply, "It's nice to see you out as well." I'm internally kicking my own ass for acting as if I don't know how to speak with a man.

"Can we go someplace quieter to chat?" he asks.

I agree so fast that I admonish myself in my head: I sound too eager.

We walk out to the back patio that is lit only by tiki torches, a fire pit and hanging string lights. It sets an intimate mood. Maurice and I sit near the fire pit to chat. He's handsy, running his hand up and down my thigh, but I don't mind. We talk about our work. We share about hobbies, places that we've visited, and places that we want to go. The music changes and a song with a slower tempo plays. Maurice slides closer to me and puts his arm behind me, resting it on the back of the loveseat. I look up at him, our eyes meet, I can tell that something is about to go down.

Maurice leans towards me, looking me square in the eyes. He licks his lips and continues towards my face. His lips touch mine. I pucker my lips slightly and we exchange the most passionate kiss I've had in a long while. It starts slow and deliberate, a couple of pecks before parting our lips to allow our tongues to meet. Still slow and concentrated, no rush, no worries about who may see us, we kiss deep. He cups my face, I push against him and grab his bald head. Now there are short moans of enjoyment, he rubs my back with one hand while his other hand remains planted on my face.

We kiss for what feels like a long time and as if we were made to kiss each other. It's like a familiar dance with an unfamiliar partner. Somehow, he knows what I need and meets that need effortlessly and without direction. He eases from my mouth and plants soft kisses on my neck, one hand in my hair, the other still rubbing my back. This man is a pleaser, passionate and intentional. It's like the Latin dancers I've seen on TV, sexy and sensual in their movements. This dance could most definitely lead to something. I exhale and ...

DING DONG ...

Awoken by the Amazon delivery, my steamy fantasy ends. *What was that all about,* I think. This man and I have not had any significant encounters. I know nothing about him except that he is a dentist and single father. I don't even know if he has a woman in his life. I mean, the kids have a mother I'm sure, but what's up there? I know nothing, but here I am having mid-day "nap dreams" about exchanging the most passionate of kisses. I'm confused. I don't know how to feel or what to think. Do I say something to him? Do I attempt to explore my fantasy? Do I act as if I didn't just dream up a near erotic encounter? I need to chill out and get out of the house for a minute. I call up my "always down and ready to ride" friend for lunch. And, true to form, she says she will be ready in an hour.

I pick Chaz up for lunch and she looks as if she has already had a couple of drinks before I arrive. She jumps in the car, her carefree flair that I have come to admire, and says to me, "Hey girl hey."

We enjoy the short drive to our favorite dive bar. It looks like a hole in the wall on the outside, but has a spacious, modern, and savvy interior. This place makes the best street tacos and drinks. We already know what we want before getting out of my car.

It's not packed like usual on a Saturday afternoon, so we get the rare opportunity to dine on the covered and screened patio. This is the only patio that Chaz & I approve of in the disrespectful heat. With pollen still falling and temperatures on the rise, this is actually a cool and clean outdoor space. The music playing is low, but definitely matches our vibe.

The faint harmonizing of Next singing "Too Close" has Chaz chair-dancing as the waiter approaches. Her spirit is contagious and when he catches a glimpse of her doing her thing, he bops towards our table only amplifying her energy. "Ladies, how are we? Are we celebrating?" he asks.

I reply with a giggle, "no, just here for lunch and great drinks."

Chaz co-signs, "That's right, bring the drinks and keep this musical vibe, we love it!"

He asks for our drink orders and smirks at Chaz's continued wiggling. "I'll have two long Island Ice Teas, please." I side eye my friend with the intention of asking what troubles she's trying to drown. Then I order a peach sangria.

The waiter leaves just as D'Angelo's "Cruising" starts to play. Chaz is now studying the menu, which is interesting because we spoke about our order in the car.

I place my menu down and check in with my friend, "Are you ok?" I ask.

"Yes, I'm good. Why do you ask?" she asks, slow winding in her chair.

"You just ordered two drinks at once."

She chuckles and explains, "oh that's because I don't want to wait and I already know I'm gonna have two."

We laugh and I start with the small talk about her morning. I don't want to jump right in with the dream that is taking up so much of my mental space because I also don't want to be interrupted by the waiter when he returns with our drinks and takes our orders. Chaz shares how her morning was and what her husband was off doing. She asks, "So what's up with you? How was your morning?" just as the waiter returns. He places our drinks on the table, Chaz jumps right in with her first drink as I order our table dip and the taco platter. This is our go-to order. We also encourage others to get this platter. Two each of carne asada, shrimp, and fish tacos with a chili lime salsa atop homemade soft corn tortillas with a side of mango chutney. As soon as our waiter leaves, I begin to tell Chaz about my mid-day dream about the handsome dentist who works in my office building. Her eyes are as big as half dollar coins by the time I finish.

"Giiirrrlll, what do you think that means?" she asks.

"I really don't know Chaz, but I don't know how I will face him after this dream."

Our waiter returns with our tacos and dip. We jump right in with the dip and chutney. Mixing the two offers a party of sweet, spicy, and cheesy goodness. A bite of my fish taco is heaven. This deliciousness almost makes me want to close my eyes and forget about the good dentist.

Chaz suggests between chews, "Your dream may mean something."

I frown, take a sip of my sangria and ask her what she means.

"Like," Chaz continues, "maybe it's your subconscious telling you to step your game up and talk to the man instead of lusting after him."

"Ok, subconscious. You trying to be deep today," I tease. We both take sips of our drinks. Maybe Chaz has a point. I go on to tell her how sharing the elevator with him, smelling his cologne does something to me. I close my eyes remembering one such occasion and chills take over my body.

I open my eyes to see Chaz giggling. She diverts her eyes to something behind me. I want to turn to see what has her attention, but there is no need. What has Chaz's attention is now standing at our table. It's Maurice. He's standing right next to us.

"Good afternoon," he says, his voice deep, rich and sexy like dark chocolate. Chaz just smiles with her drink straw sitting on her bottom lip.

I introduce them, "Chaz this is Maurice. Maurice, Chaz."

"Oh this is the guy from the dream," Chaz blurts out.

I am shook. I am embarrassed.

"Dream?" Maurice inquires, "What dream?"

I lower my gaze. Chaz takes a long swallow of her drink, avoiding my eyes. I have to find words, but not many come to mind.

"I'll have to tell you about it one day," I manage to get out.

Maurice smirks and looks me square in the eyes and says, "I look forward to it." Before walking off to his table, he lightly brushes his hand on my shoulder. *Oh my!*

Chaz and I continue our lunch chatting about various things from business ideas to vacations. I half-hear Chaz because I am lost in the thoughts of what just occurred. *I can't believe Chaz outed me.*

I look up and behind Chaz, I notice that Maurice is seated two tables over and is facing me. He's looking right at me. *Could something be there?* He has to be thinking something.

I return my attention to my table just as Chaz asks, "What's your therapist's name? I have someone that really needs her assistance."

I dig in my crossbody for Dr. Andrea Sims's card and hand it to Chaz. She must notice that my presence at this table is barely there, my mind is all over the place, because she asks, "What's on your mind, Tab? Ever since that dentist walked in, you've been all in your head."

"Girl, I had a mid-day dream about him that was mad steamy and then seeing him here has messed me up a little bit."

"Maybe you should tell him," Chaz suggests nonchalantly.

Historically I would have emphatically rejected such an idea. No way would I put myself out like that. But maybe Chaz was on to something. After all, Maurice has been stealing glances at me since he arrived. Chaz conveniently gets up to go to the restroom, leaving an opportunity for Maurice to walk over. He does exactly that.

"May I sit?" he asks.

"Sure." *Why am I so stinking nervous? We are both attractive, successful, and articulate adults. I have just as much, if not more to offer as he does.* I fidget.

Maurice interrupts my thoughts by asking, "So this dream ... I'd like to hear about it."

What the hell! I share the dream with all of the details. Maurice bites his bottom lip and nods his head. The 20 seconds of silence I received were agonizing.

He finally speaks, "Interesting because I have been wondering a few things about you too."

Oh my gosh! Don't embarrass yourself, Tab. Hold it together. "Oh yeah? Wondering what exactly?" *Yes, that was cool. Play it cool.*

Maurice twists his mouth and draws his bottom lip between his teeth. A glimpse of his pearly whites. "Thoughts that you are probably good in *every* way imaginable."

Well Damn. I need more. Tell me more. I raise one eyebrow as if to question his statement. There's no mistaking this flirting. It's assertive.

It's in your face. I nod. *I see what he's doing here.* It's like we're playing Ping-Pong ball and it's my turn. It's like a challenge. So I say, "Well there is only one way to find that out."

Maurice leans in, smirks and whispers, "You just say when." He winks and gets up to return to his table.

My mouth drops and before I can react, Chaz is back at the table. She leans in, places four of her fingers under my chin and pushes my mouth closed. She let out an "un huh" followed up with a smirk. She waves the waiter over to the table and giggles, "Check please."

A text message from my cousin Crystal interrupts the exchange. She invites me to game night at her house on Friday and, of course, Chaz is down.

The week a busy blur, I am ready for game night at my cousin's house. It is the best way to spend a Friday night. The theme for game night is "*All Black Every Thang.*" Guests were asked to dress in all black and prepare to play the "classic Black games or have your Black card revoked" per the text invite. Spectators are allowed but will be ragged big time.

My homegirl Shavonne pulls up at the same time as me. I laugh out loud because she looks like Angela Davis. This chick has blown her natural hair out to form the largest, Blackest afro I have ever seen up close. This is bound to be the most fun I've had in a while.

The plan was for Chaz and Shavonne to meet me here. Chaz beat us. I walk in to what looks like a Black Panther meet up with all of the black leather, afros, and fist hair picks. Our host, Crystal is sitting at the spades table with Chaz as her partner talking cash money shit, so that means they are winning. Crystal's boyfriend Cory is making drinks in the kitchen and talking sports with a few of the other guys.

I notice this light skinned, husky, teddy bear look-a-like that I hadn't seen before. He has a face full of freckles and a very nice smile. The beard helps a lot with the attraction I'm feeling. He notices me as well. I'm sure the black skin-tight leather pants, black asymmetrical top baring enough of my midriff to make a handsome man take notice, and the black studded red bottoms help.

He nods and bites his bottom lip, as if to signal that he likes what he sees. For the next 10 minutes, he steals glances at me that linger long enough for me to notice. I like his subtleties. The sly smiles, the biting of the lip, the lasting glances. He's definitely feeling me.

I walk over to Cory to ask for a drink. He laughs and says, "I know what you want. Crystal made sure I had a stash just for you." Cory shakes me up an Amaretto Sour just the way I like it. I don't care that all of my friends and family make fun of me for this being my go to drink for years, 20 years to be exact. If I am nothing, I am loyal.

I find a spot near the spades table to watch my cousin and best friend walk another pair straight off the table. Mr. Teddy Bear strolls over, "Hey gorgeous, I'm Charles."

He smells good. I like his voice, but I get a slight sense of a "hood boy" vibe. It's subdued, but its most definitely there. The tattoos on his neck, arms, and smell of weed paired with the way he drawled "gawgeous" are good indicators. "Hi Charles. It's nice to meet you."

Holding my hand out for a shake, he kisses it instead.

Crystal announces that it's time for Black Card Revoked. We group in three teams of five and unfortunately, Charles is not on my team, so I have to wait to find out more about him. During this game I question Crystal's selection of friends. Several are unaware of classic Black shows and many Hip Hop artists. The fact that we have to explain the wondrous Wu Tang Clan, to way too many participants, is embarrassing. Most of us are obviously very surprised by the lack of Black knowledge in a house full of Black people, that we throw the cards up and abandon the game without deciding a winning team.

I find a quiet spot to sit, take my shoes off and rest my feet in the chair next to me. Enjoying the music and singing along to "Doo Wop" by Lauryn Hill, Charles walks over, pick my feet up, sits down and lays my feet in his lap. He looks my feet over as if to look for imperfections.

I could have told him there are none. I take great care of my feet, always have.

"You look tired," he says, "Do you live far?"

"I only live 15 minutes away, Crystal is my cousin so I could stay if need be."

He simply replies with an, "mmm," and a nod.

I ask, "Why you asking, you wanna go home with me?"

In true hood dude fashion, Charles, responds with, "Hell yeah."

I don't know why I asked that, knowing good and damn well that I wasn't going take this strange man home with me. He doesn't press the issue and asks for my phone number. We exchanged numbers and he proceeds to tell me, "I'm the man that you need."

What? I laugh a little bit, "Is that so?"

Charles nods. Smiles and walks off. There was no further explanation, he just walks away. Now I have always been an inquisitive person. I thirst for knowledge of any kind and appreciate a good understanding.

I slip my pumps back on and follow him. Sliding past several people standing around holding red Solo cups, I catch up to Charles just as he steps over the threshold of the patio door. I tap him on the shoulder, "Excuse me, sir." We both make it out to the warm night air.

"You don't have to be so formal," he states in a Southern drawl.

"I wouldn't call it formal just polite," I retort.

"Polite, huh?" he asks with a slight smirk.

It seems as if he likes a little back and forth. Charles pulls out a Newport and lights up. Blowing out his first puff, he asks "You single?"

"Yep. You?"

"Something like that," he says evasively, blowing out smoke, careful not to blow in my direction.

"What does that mean?" *Girl, do you really care?* If he can't give a clear answer, I'm not sure if I should even be entertaining him. I must admit though that he is cute and the rough edges intrigue me. *Tab, what are you even doing out here with this man?*

"I have a few lady friends. No one that I see exclusively, but a couple have been around for some time. I'd like to get to know you though." Another drag of the cancer stick. "A woman like you may make me let the rest go."

Bullshit! "Oh, don't stop the things you were doing before meeting me," I respond watching him finish his cigarette. The fact that he smokes is a turn off for me, so I can't say for certain why I'm still out here talking to him.

"So can I go home with you as you suggested?" Charles asks.

My eyes buck at his boldness. *Uh no. I was just fucking around, dude!* I'm at a loss for words.

Charles laughs and says, "I guess not."

He pulls a pack of gum from his pocket and walks over to the patio loveseat. He motions for me to join him, patting a space next to him. I do, although I'm still not quite sure why I am entertaining this man.

We talk for a good while. He's pretty interesting actually. While he is definitely a little on the hood side, he has a degree in engineering that he doesn't use because he's not much of a "corporate cat." He owns a detail business that has large contracts with several area car dealerships. He makes good money and admits that most people assume it's "dope money" because of his past. Charles admits that he sold drugs for many years, but after his cousin was killed seven years ago, he decided to quit. He also admits to smoking weed daily and will occasionally put "a homie in contact with a connect," but that is the extent of his illegal activities "these days." He shares that he gets a little kickback from making such connections, but is "no longer in the game." The conversation almost ended when I shared that I'm an attorney. We laugh and he motions for me to lay my feet in his lap again. A foot massage on my cousin's patio is unexpected, but much appreciated.

The day after game night is a blur, and I sleep most all day on Sunday. When I'm not asleep, I am curled up on my sectional with fuzzy socks, my bonnet, and my weighted blanket, watching documentaries on Netflix. I want wings, but don't want to get out to get them, so I order in. I talk with Charles periodically throughout the weekend. Still questioning why I was giving him my time and attention. I also exchange texts with Maurice.

Monday arrives too fast. I walk into my office building to join the line in the coffee shop on the first floor, not bothering to take my sunglasses off. At the head of the line, I spot Maurice. I lower my head out of embarrassment from the admission of the salacious dream about him and the extremely flirtatious phone calls and texts we have been engaging in.

I hadn't seen him since I told him about the dream. Speaking on the phone and texting gave me a sense of protection, cover, but being in his presence, after all that we've been sharing, is causing a shyness that I hadn't felt in a while. *Keyboard thugging!* I had been bold over the phone, but now my nerves give me a queasy feeling.

I notice that he is preoccupied with his phone. I was relieved. *Maybe he didn't see me.* I reach the front of the line to order my usual and there was a cup with my name on it sitting on the counter.

The young lady behind the counter says, "Dr. Jones paid for your drink."

OMG, he did see me. I smile politely, take the drink and head towards the elevators. Once again feeling relief in taking the ride to the ninth floor alone. I don't know what to say just yet.

Dr. Maurice Jones's practice was on the seventh floor and I'm hoping that the elevator doesn't stop on that floor. I want to get to my office as quickly as possible. The doors open to the ninth floor right into the lobby of my firm.

I walk fast towards my office in an attempt to avoid people this early in the morning, but my assistant catches up to me with a briefing marked *URGENT.* I roll my eyes, take the envelope and leave her just outside my office door at her desk.

"Please hold my calls for the next couple of hours so that I can get through this," I request holding the stiff envelope. Sloane agrees.

I plop down behind my desk and open the envelope. It's not a briefing at all, it's a contract for an account I reviewed. This is just informational, so I don't know why it's marked *URGENT.* I take a few deep breaths to lower my blood pressure. I have two uninterrupted hours so I close my eyes and continue with a relaxing meditation, I easily slip into a daydream about Maurice and Charles.

They have both expressed interest. I communicated with each of them over the weekend and they both seem equally attracted to me. These men are very different and there is a draw to both. The attraction to Maurice is obvious, Charles, on the other hand is rooted in curiosity.

My thoughts are interrupted by Sloane telling me that my two hours are up and she has more contracts for my review. I ended up being busier than I anticipated and before I knew it, Sloane was bringing me lunch that I had not ordered. She sat a ten piece wing dinner in front of me, mango habanero and teriyaki wings, mixed veggies, and an iced tea. I smile as this is the exact meal I had on Sunday. This is also the exact meal that I told Charles that I was having when he called asking to take me out for Sunday dinner. Just as I rose to wash my hands, my phone chimes with a text alert. It's Charles asking if I had gotten my lunch. I reply that I had and was just about to dig in. He simply responded "*cool.*"

What are you doing, Tabitha? I can't help but wonder.

The remainder of the day moved along quickly and I typically do not work late on Mondays, but I was in a good groove. I had told Sloane she could go home an hour ago; I really need to be doing the same. I gather my belongings and head for the door. I wait for the elevator while texting my cousin that I worked late and am headed home. I like to let someone know my whereabouts when alone and off schedule.

The doors to the elevator open as she responds asking me to call her when I make it inside of my car. I look up and see Maurice. A tad confused because the floor to his offices are below mine. Apparently he could read the surprise on my face because he immediately explained, "Hey, I walked out to my car and saw that yours was still here and figured I'd come check on you. Everything good?"

"Yes." Still stunned to see his gorgeous face before me. "I had several documents to review and didn't want them hanging."

"May I walk you to your car?" he asks.

I agree and step onto the elevator. Standing an entire foot taller than me, I have to look up to see if he is looking at me. He is, and I blush. *Oh my goodness!*

He compliments my outfit, and I compliment his cologne. I close my eyes while doing so. Noticing my reaction, he grabs my hand and pulls me closer to him.

He leans down and out of habit, I stand on my tip toes. My head tilted back to provide him full access to my lips, he kisses me. My fantasies about him are being realized. His lips are soft. He plants several tender kisses on my lips before pulling me into him for a deeper kiss. I moan and reach up for his bald head. Maurice holds my right hand, his left arm firmly wrapped around my waist. His kisses are intentional, aimed to please. *It's like the dream!*

The elevator dings as we arrive at the lobby. The withdrawal is slow, almost reluctant. The bulge in his slacks affirm his enjoyment. Maurice slowly releases my waist, steps back and adjusts himself. There are no words, just slight looks of surprise. I could see how easy it would be to lose control with him. There is definitely physical chemistry.

He breaks the silence and takes me away from my thoughts, "That was good."

We step off of the elevator.

I agree, nodding my head, wanting more and unable to form intelligent words. We walk slowly to my car. I use the remote to unlock the driver's side door and Maurice grabs the handle to open it for me.

More silence and intense looks.

I smile a half smile and tell him goodnight. He nods and says the same.

The rest of the week is filled with work, texts with Charles and stolen moments with Maurice in the office.

This continues for three weeks.

It's Friday night and I am home alone, excited that I have nothing to do. I'm exhausted.

I've been juggling Maurice and Charles for a month now. Most times, I'm noncommittal and other times, I give in to one and then the other to keep a little balance. I honestly can't see how some people date multiple people at one time. This shit is exhausting. I've gone out with both Charles and Maurice several times, a couple of times occurred within a day or two of each other. Interestingly enough, we all agree that a relationship is not the immediate goal and that we are just "getting to know each other."

Part of me wonders if these men think I am capable of maintaining things simply as they are. It is popular belief that women typically soon wonder "where is this going" after so long. My time to ask that question had likely passed. There are no expectations, I'm just winging it. Just having fun, I tell myself on a regular basis. *What guy wouldn't be cool with that?*

Now I learned my lesson long ago, I will not sleep with more than one man at a time. Having near misses of sexual encounters with Maurice, cancels the opportunity for Charles. I remember each time we have kissed and each time is more intense than the last.

I can feel the arousal growing at the thought of it. I bite my bottom lip and consider using my massager for relief. "What are you doing, Tab?" I ask myself aloud. Sometimes my internal conflict is literally like two people outside of myself, removed from my physical being while I watch from above. Tabitha and Tab debate whether or not I am too old to behave in such a manner.

To be entertaining two men just because I can with no intention to do any more than what we are doing, is plain crazy. My curiosity got me here. Being curious about the professional and handsome man in my office building and intrigued by the "hood dude" I met at a house party.

See Maurice is the guy that many women say they want. Good looking, professional, successful, responsible, clean cut, respectable and respectful are all qualities on the list of the ideal man. He has them all. You know, the marrying type.

Charles is the complete opposite. He's a straight up, unmistakable, hood dude. Not tattoos-on-the-face-and-a-gold-grill hood, but familiar with jail and how to flip some shit hood.

Two complete opposites. One drives an Audi A8 and the other drives a matte black Charger with black rims and a custom sound system. One I can see myself actually entertaining for more than a couple of months, if a relationship was the goal; the other I'd never take around my family for fear they would commit me to a psychiatric hospital.

Maurice is the type of man who would make me a hot toddy when I'm sick and stay with me until I sweated out any illness inhabiting my body. Charles is the type of man to recommend that I smoke a blunt and take a couple of shots of Hennessy and holla at him in a few days. They are not at all the same.

While on the one hand, I know that I don't want anything serious with anyone at this time; curiosity is distracting me with thoughts of bedding Maurice. Right now, curiosity has me in some entanglement type shit. We have literally done just about everything but penetrative sex. Our efforts to stay away from a bedroom in hopes that we wouldn't go too far have proven futile. I have allowed Maurice to eat me out in his office one evening after the offices were clear of anyone who could catch us. It was stupid, I know, but it was also so exhilarating. The thought of possibly getting caught having sex at work excited me. I came three times just from him going down on me. Maurice took his time that night. He maneuvered his tongue as if he had tasted the folds below before. He passionately kissed my yoni as if it were his life's purpose to do so.

"Hmmmph," I say aloud remembering that night. Now Charles has flat out asked to "eat the pussy," Just like that, "Eat. The. Pussy." The fact that he says it that way turns me off and is enough for me to pass on that. He could be a pussy connoisseur, but his approach needs work for me to find out.

It's a rainy Saturday and I plan for it to be a lazy Saturday. My phone was on Do Not Disturb all night so I woke to several text messages from Charles. I hadn't spoken to him in a few days and hadn't really been all that responsive. My plan is to just fade away, but he isn't making that easy.

Yesterday 10:43 PM

Tabitha, Why I ain't heard from you? You good?

Tab?

Today 8:13 AM

It's fckd up that you won't txt me bck or answer yo phone. I'm jst making sure you straight

Today 10:15 AM

Fck it! Do you.

At least let me knw you cool.

Tab?

Today 2:32 PM

Mane, say something

TAB!!!!

I should probably let him know that we have run our course. I've just been so preoccupied with Maurice that I hadn't wanted to even have the conversation with Charles. Too many things have been a turn off and having Mr. Near Perfect doing so many things right, I just as well fade to black with Charles. My phone now ringing, I take my time grabbing it off the coffee table assuming it's Charles. It's actually Maurice.

"Hello?"

"Hey beautiful. You staying dry?" His voice is intoxicating. It's like a smooth brandy.

He set up the perfect opportunity for me to be nasty and flirtatious, "I am, but I'd rather be wet with you."

"Mmmm. I bet I can make that happen."

"How would you make that happen?"

"I can show you better than I can tell you. What's on your agenda today?"

The reactions that this man can produce by merely speaking should be illegal, "I'm lounging today. What about you?"

"Right now, I'm waiting to see if my son's game will be cancelled and then I will know better how to plan."

I love the idea of Maurice coming over to wet me up because I know that he can so well, but I am enjoying my down time watching documentaries and eating junk. "Well spend the time with your son, there will be plenty opportunities for us."

"Will there be?"

"I'm sure, Maurice. Take care of daddy duties today. Text or call when you can."

"Will do beautiful. Enjoy your time."

And with that, my lounging continues. The calls and texts from Charles finally stop and I've completed two of the three documentaries that I planned for today. My snacking has been crazy. An empty bag of kettle corn popcorn and three empty 20oz water bottles litter my coffee table.

I'm deep in a pint of Haagen-Dazs peach sorbet when my text chime goes crazy. Six back to back messages from Chaz. Three pictures of Maurice sitting in the bleachers of a gym very close to a woman barely clothed followed by three text messages so filled with expletives that I can't understand what she's trying to say. A final chime of a message that asks, "Want me to roll up on him?"

Lesson 14: Therapy

I moved my session to today, Monday because my weekend was so full of conflicting emotions. It's still raining and my mood is still lazy, has been since Saturday. I need to process the weekend. I need to speak with Dr. Drea about Maurice, Charles, and my indecisiveness.

Upon entering Dr. Drea's office, I notice that she has a new name tag on the outside door. **Dr. Andrea J. Sims, LCSW-S, PhD**. I don't know why that catches my eye. Perhaps because I hadn't seen it before. It's new. Different.

I enter the therapy space and take my usual seat and notice that the amethyst box is gone. I'm a little disappointed. Another change noted.

"Hi Tabitha. How's it going? I don't think I've seen you so comfortably dressed."

I didn't go to work today, so I'm dressed down in a grey jogging suit and white Air Max. Another change from my norm when I visit Dr. Drea.

"I've been better, Doc."

"Are you ill?"

"No ma'am, just heavy. Emotional. I couldn't go through the week carrying so much."

"Ok, well let's begin shall we. Start with whatever you feel most comfortable."

I take a deep breath and look for something else to focus on since the beautiful box is not here. "Dr. Drea, I don't know what I'm doing anymore. For a while I've entertained two men, Maurice and Charles. These men are very different and we were all on the same page that we were just getting to know each other. Well as time went on, I started to enjoy my interactions with Maurice more and I stopped communication with Charles."

"Ok." Dr. Drea nods.

"The interesting thing is that I felt that neither of these situations would go anywhere. I don't even want anything serious right now, with anyone. Hell, I don't even want anything casual right now. I have asked myself multiple times 'what are you doing', but I never have a coherent answer. I also don't stop what I'm doing."

I share more of my self-imposed dramatic dilemma with Dr. Drea. I give her all the details to bring her up to speed. She has a unique way of telling me about myself with a nice dose of spiritually-aligned perspective. I could use a good read from her today.

"Have you had sex with Maurice", she asks.

"Not penetrative sex, but I have allowed him to perform oral sex," I answer matter-of-factly.

"What's stopping you from going further?"

"I honestly don't know. I feel like it depends on the day and if the wind blows a certain way," I answer honestly. I realize when I say it aloud that it sounds like utter stupidity. The truth of the matter is that Maurice is capable of arousing me. I enjoy the things that he has done to me, the reactions he has been able to produce. I believe that it would only get better.

"How far did things get with Charles?"

"Oh there was nothing physical there. He was just someone to talk to."

"Ok. So Tabitha, I'm a little confused. When we started with the journals, the goals was to revisit past lessons to refresh your memory of the things you have learned throughout your romantic life in an attempt to avoid similar mistakes. How does this situation move you closer to that goal?"

"I don't know Dr. Drea."

"Oh no. Remember that we don't use that phrase. We think here. We dig deep and figure things out."

I knew what her response would be before I allowed that phrase to leave my mouth. I twiddle with my fingers. "I was just doing something and fucked around and caught feelings for Maurice." I tell her about the pictures that Chaz sent to me and how I felt I had been cheated on when I'm not even in a relationship.

"I hate to hear that your feelings are hurt, but let's take a step back and let me ask this, do you have that kind of time?"

Huh? This is like a rhetorical question, a set up where she will lead me down a road of uncomfortable hard truths and realizations that will likely make me want to leave. I won't leave. I never do. Sometimes I call her Dr. Dre for how she produces logical thought from my mess. The way she does it makes me feel like I am on death row. There is silence. The therapeutic silence that she uses so well.

I finally ask for clarification, "What do you mean?"

"Do you have the kind of time to do things for the sake of having something to do? Things that you do not value and that provide no value to you? Do you have the time to do things that you're not even sure you want to do? Things that bring you no honor? Do you have the time to be allowing your feelings to be hurt by a man that you aren't even dating for real? In a previous session, you spoke about the things you ultimately want in your life. How does moving with no intention move you closer to those things?"

She went in on me, but she is right. I know the answers. Just like I know what I want and don't want. "No, I don't have that kind of time, Dr. Drea and I know that by entertaining these men with no intentions of being anything at all, will not bring me closer to what I want in my life. The craziest part of all of this is that I am not bored; or lonely; or desperate. I have considered if all of this is because I do eventually want companionship. That desire is likely why I'm all in my feelings about seeing pictures of Maurice with another woman. I mean I know we aren't in a relationship, but damn." *Whew!*

"So what is this all about, Tabitha?" Dr. Drea asks.

"That's what I need you to help me figure out, Dr. Drea," I admit. More fidgeting I finally admit, "Maybe I am afraid to commit again. I long for companionship, but only if I can stay safe."

"Ok, so how does *that* work?"

"It doesn't. It's not."

"Ok, Tabitha, lets pick this thing apart. Tell me about each of these men and what purpose they serve or served in getting what you ultimately want. What are you learning?"

A deep breath to brace myself for full transparency, "So with Charles, he kind of reminded me of someone from my past that I was into, but I knew with my entire being that he was no good. So maybe that situation is more nostalgic, like maybe having a second chance to experience something I thought I wanted years ago. With Maurice, he's literally the ideal man that women fantasize about having. I fantasize about having this type of man, at least. He has many of the qualities that are on my list of the qualities that I want in a man. It's intriguing, I suppose, to see my list in human form, live, breathing and in color."

I pause and consider her question about their purpose. Dr. Drea, in her comfort zone of quietness, of silence, she allows me the space to sit with what I just said. We sit there enveloped by the stillness while I search for an answer more acceptable than *I don't know*. It feels like 20 minutes have passed with neither of us saying a thing. It's likely only been about 45 seconds. I open my mouth to speak and then stop. I look at Dr. Drea and then back at my hands. *Where's the amethyst box?*

"The lesson I suppose is that of valuing my worth and understanding the totality of my being and what I hope to attract. Maybe the purpose of this situation was to make me uncomfortable enough to realize this lesson." I'm sure that sounds like pure gibberish. Hell it doesn't make sense to me right now.

Dr. Drea leans in and asks, "Explain further, please."

It is as if she senses that I am on the precipice of some type of realization that will make everything make sense.

To my left, on the table on the side of the loveseat opposite where I normally set my water, I spot the amethyst box and smile. It's like that box comforts me.

"See, it's like I made this list of the type of man that I want in my life. The list contains physical characteristics; emotional characteristics and capabilities; financial status and professional standing; and even the spiritual. While Maurice may check 95% of those boxes, some part of me is waiting for the other shoe to fall. Maybe it's the woman in the photo. Maybe she's that shoe." I shrug my shoulders. "So a part of me is fearful of Maurice. Like I made the list, but didn't actually consider what would happen if I actually got it. Maybe I never really believed I deserved the man I dreamed of. And to have him at my fingertips ... " *What's the word?* "It's daunting. It's like seeing that woman is like 'see I knew something was up.' My initial response was one of protection. I wanted to cut him off. But then again, I wonder if I am giving things between us enough time, attention, and energy to even develop. I want to believe that I am worthy of a man who has every good thing on that list. I want to wholeheartedly trust my intuition. I want the relationship I've always said I wanted."

I feel a tinge of pride within myself. The fact that I am articulating my internal struggle is big for me. This, unfortunately, is a lesson that seems to resurface every so often. It's like a perm that just won't take. I learn the lessons and begin to feel worthy of everything I want and desire, then comes along a fucked up situation that makes me second guess everything. Makes me want to pull back. One step forward, three steps back.

Dr. Drea holds space for me to ramble. I continue, "I feel like I have romanticized the whole 'falling in love' thing and when things don't fit into my made up paradigm, I dismiss it all. It's like I know I need to shift my thinking. Like I know my worth and can verbalize it much of the time, but do I really value it? Like do I *really* believe it? Do I understand how worthy I actually am?"

"That's amazing Tabitha. Stop ignoring that you know your worth. Connect to that sense of worthiness often so that there is no question about how worthy you are. So that you believe wholeheartedly that you have always been worthy of everything that you desire. You'll be less likely to dishonor yourself." Dr. Drea pauses. "Maybe the feeling that you have that Maurice 'isn't the one' has more to do with self-sabotage born from feelings of unworthiness than it does with the 5% that you say is missing."

Hmm. "That is something to really think about."

"Have you inquired about the woman in the photo?"

I hadn't. "No. My immediate response was to ghost him, but I know that wouldn't be easy."

Dr. Drea posed several good points that I need to sit with and truly consider. It won't kill me to have a conversation with Maurice. To have an understanding. To give understanding. I've also come to realize that sometimes the development of a real relationship takes time. Maybe that is what Maurice and I need, more time.

Lesson 15: Mike & Maurice

I assume that in any given woman's life, she has constructed her perfect man over and over again. I know I have many times over. I made a list, revised it several times. I've rewritten it and revised it again. Taking the best qualities of this man and the most admirable traits of that man, balling them up to mold The Man. Several of the important qualities have consistently made the list. Each failed relationship and the lessons I've learned from each prompted me to add new qualities and take away outdated ones. I can really see the evolution of my choice in men by looking back at those lists. My list grew to be four pages at one point.

As I've matured, I've revised it down to two. It is two pages of the most important qualities I want and need in a life partner. I believe in being specific. After all, with everything I've been through, I deserve everything I'm manifesting and more. Throughout my life, I thought I had found him a few times, only to be disappointed and taught another lesson about love and love loss.

If I am completely honest, I played a major role in my relationship failings as well. In my youth, and often times in my haste for a relationship, I attempted to mold myself into the person that the guy I was dating wanted. I compromised on some things, covered up parts of me just to appeal to him, and overlooked a lot just to keep the image alive. Over time, I started to lose sight of who I really was. It's crazy to sit back and think over my seasons of love. In doing so, there were times I didn't recognized the woman playing me. She sure wasn't the real me. Taking an objective look at my relationships helped me see that.

My representative showed up for far too long. It's that "best foot forward" mentality where people only show the best parts of themselves to impress or appease someone else. The representative is when people attempt to highlight qualities that they never really fully possessed in order to keep an image, even a perceived one, alive. It's like code switching. My representative was a shapeshifter. She was bold and confident at times; then shy and observant other times. She could and did morph into the woman whichever guy she was dating wanted at that time, my representative was versatile.

Now, there were glimpses of the real me present, but fear of judgement prevented me from walking fully in my own being in most relationships. If the real Tabitha stood up and wasn't received well, she shrank and the representative would emerge. Often times, the fear of rejection or ridicule kept the real Tabitha at bay totally. It's long overdue for the real me to show up 100% of the time now. The authentic me can no longer idly standby while the representative fucks up another relationship. I've come to realize that I don't always feel confident or outgoing and that is ok. The lesser confident times do not detract from me as a person and certainly do not mean that I lack confidence.

So here I am, seeing Maurice more regularly. Following my last therapy session, I decided to initiate the difficult conversation of expectations and to inquire about the woman. Turns out, she is the mother of his son there to watch the game. *Go figure.*

I also decide to talk to Charles. I figure I owe him the maturity of a conversation instead of ghosting him. I tell him that things aren't working out and I don't feel the need to explain why I made such a decision. I had to listen to him moan and complain about me leading him on and about how he "fed" me good. *Negro, a woman needs more than a high dollar salad and wings from time to time.*

Maurice and I continue to hang out. Not as frequently as before, and I often remind myself that we were just getting to know each other.

Taking it slow and slow is ok. I don't need to rush anything. He accepts the casual nature of what we were doing. He isn't applying pressure or advocating for more. This allowed space for Charles to merely be replaced.

A Saturday out with my girls, I meet Mike. It's invigorating. I like him instantly. We meet at a hookah bar the weekend of a coworker's wedding and he is out to unwind after a benefit golf tournament. I notice him looking at me and a couple of my friends as we laugh, chair dance, and gush over the pictures we took at the selfie station during the reception. He's surely a handsome man. Smooth honey skin, bald head, salt and pepper beard, giving him a distinguished look. He's definitely nice on the eyes. Almost looks like Maurice.

"Come on Tab, try it," Crystal says, handing me the hookah tube, breaking my eye contact with Mike. While I am surely too old for peer pressure, I have wanted to try hookah for quite some time. My girls are old pros at it. Chaz even has one at her house.

"You have to inhale deep, but don't swallow," Chaz instructs.

I do as instructed and immediately begin coughing. I am no smoker of any kind, so this is all new to me. They laugh and tell me to keep trying. The way my throat burns, I think I'm good on that.

I look up and see that Mike has his hand over his mouth as if to suppress a laugh. I tilt my head as if to ask "really" and he smiles. It's a beautiful smile and it looks like he takes good care of his teeth. I know the smile of years in braces. I own a product of one. Again, I am reminded of Maurice.

I smile back and think that his first impression of me will be my amateur hookah skills. And for a split second I feel embarrassed. I feel judged. Immediately my representative wants to take charge as she has done so many times before, to put up a front that I am perfect, that no embarrassing moments occur in my life. Ever ready to perpetrate a lie!

I reach for the hookah tube again with the idea that by the time I leave here tonight I will be a pro at this smoking through a tube thing. *Who's this for?* I don't have time to ponder this notion¾I'm in the middle of what should be a good time with my girls and a meeting with a handsome man. I begin to think of ways that I could introduce myself to him. *Should I keep making eye contact in hopes that he would catch a clue and come over? Should I send him a drink or would that make him feel less than a man? Should one of my girls play my wing woman?*

Just as I was about to continue the agonizing internal questioning, the waitress brings over a drink and a note for me. She pointed at the Maurice look-a-like and said, "From him."

I look up, he waves. It's like he read my mind. My attention returns to the table and I realize that another four eyes are staring at me.

"Well what does it say?" Crystal asks.

I open the folded napkin to find a phone number under the name "Mike."

"It's a phone number," I reply, showing the napkin to the ladies. The internal mutterings begin again. *Am I really expected to call him first? Surely an independent woman such as myself isn't worried about the thoughts and opinions of others.* I stop myself and smile. I am at a loss for words. This has never happened before. Before I could get too deep in my mind, Chaz interrupts my thoughts, "You gonna drink that?"

I honestly hadn't thought anymore about the drink that the waitress said was from Mike. After all, I didn't know what it was. I wave for the waitress and point at the tall glass, "What is this?"

"He said to just bring you what you were already drinking and he'd pay for it. I can ask the bartender though," she said with a smile.

"She's not gonna drink it," Crystal says turning to Chaz.

"Shit I will!" Chaz replies. We all laugh.

By the end of the night, I didn't see Mike at the bar anymore. We ask for the tab and gather our things. We were informed that the ticket had been paid by the gentleman who sent over the last drink. I mentally tallied up our tickets and in drinks alone, that was over $150. We also had appetizers and hookah, all of which were paid for by Mr. Mike.

"Impressive," Crystal states.

"Mmmhmmm," Chaz says.

We had all driven separately as that is how we arrived to the wedding. My car is parked two spaces from Chaz so we walk arm and arm. We hear, "Excuse me, pretty lady in the red pumps."

I look down to double check what I wore and realize that he's speaking to me. I turn to see Mike's smiling face. I stop to allow him to reach to me. A slight jog gets him to me quicker than I anticipated and before my mind could start in on evaluating what was going on.

He stopped a few feet shy of me, "Hey. I'm Mike," he says and extends his hand. I take it and tell him my name to which he responded with a half-smile.

"Thanks for the drink."

"Did your friend enjoy it?" he asks obviously having noticed that I didn't drink it.

I smile, "Yes. Yes, she did. I had already reached my limit for the evening, so I thought best that I didn't partake."

I wave Crystal and Chaz off and lean against my car. Mike and I stood outside of the hookah bar talking and getting to know each other. I learned that Mike recently moved to the area after his parents retired and moved away from his home town. He felt that with them gone and his siblings long gone, there was no reason for him to stick around. He's a blue collar guy with a healthy appreciation for a tailored suit and self-care. His hands, and admittedly his feet, are manicured. His facial hair is well maintained and he reports that he shaves his "baby soft" head every other day. I'm seriously impressed. I want to feel the softness for myself, but don't want to send the wrong impression. From what I hear, rubbing on a man's bald head does something to him and could start something I had no intentions on finishing.

We talk as if we have known each other for years. As random as most of the conversation has been, it feels organic and safe. Enough to want to continue to converse at a later time.

He asks for my phone number and if we could have lunch the next day. I agree and he opens my car door as he says, "Be safe getting home and I'll call to finalize lunch plans."

I agree and enter my car. I drive home in near silence trying to keep from overthinking things. I was impressed by Mike's initiative. That's something that I really wanted from Maurice. Mike was intentional and that's huge these days. In a time where a person's true intentions are rarely stated or even known, it's refreshing to meet a man who can express his interest up front. He was a gentleman and certainly knew how to leave an impression. That night, I actually went to sleep smiling at the possibilities.

My phone rings at 10am. "Hello?"

"Good morning, beautiful. It's Mike. I'm just calling to give you the details of our lunch plans. I have everything planned and all you have to do is meet me at Dave and Busters on the West side of town at noon."

"Ok?" I think to myself, *planned?*

Attempting to reassure me, Mike ends the call with "It'll be a chill vibe, promise."

I agree, "Ok."

Seeing as how we are meeting at what I consider a large arcade, I dress very casual in jeans, an off the shoulder light sweater and Air Max. I let the magnificent Whitney Houston sing to me about dancing with somebody as I get myself together. My 80s/90s playlist shuffling on my Amazon Music never ceases to surprise me with the classics that get me moving and singing.

I put the finishing touches on my high bun while swaying and singing about good love. This music has me in such a good mood that I continue with the station in my car. I thoroughly enjoy my mini concert of Anita Baker and Whitney Houston during the 20 minute drive to my destination.

I pull into the parking lot, just past the entrance I see Mike standing outside waiting for me. He's dressed in slim cut dark jeans, a

Rolling Stones T-shirt, and what looks to be a pair of black Cole Hann sneakers. I smile at his outfit. He walks to my car as I pull into a spot and proceeds to open my door. I get out and am greeted with a side hug. We walk together and he asks, "You ready to have a good time?"

I nod and smile, unsure of what to expect. This is very different from any lunch date I have had in the past. Mike reaches for my hand as we walk the short distance to the entrance. His hands are soft, yet manly. Mike takes care of the business at the counter while I stand aside waiting to hear his ideas for the day. Nervousness creeps up and a tinge of guilt as if I'm betraying Maurice. *Come on Tab, get it together.*

"So, what's the game plan?" I ask looking up at him. He's not as tall as Maurice, but he's most definitely taller than me.

"I figured we'd play a few games. Let me see how competitive you are. We will have a few drinks, maybe an appetizer or two while I brag about beating you." He smiles and winks, "I'm thinking we will spend about an hour or two here and then head to an early dinner. After dinner, there's a comedy show uptown that I'd like us to take in."

This man really has my entire day *and* night planned out. As if to read my mind, Mike says, "I just want to be around you for as long as I can. If I'm honest, I felt something last night that I can't explain and I figured that if I get an opportunity to spend a significant amount of time in your presence, then I would figure out what that something was."

"So this is some sort of experiment?" I ask and immediately regret it. The last time that I made an assumption about a man's intentions with me, it was the demise of the relationship. I certainly didn't want to repeat that and mess things up with Mike before we could get started good.

I am shocked by his response, "Well ... I suppose that's one way to look at it. Yes! As much of an experiment as any date would be in the beginning of a courtship. I mean, I felt a connection last night. I like you and enjoyed your company. I wanted to take you out to see if that feeling was a one off or if the same feeling continues on a new day."

This man can give an intelligent, well thought answer on the fly! "Ok."

We play skeeball, air hockey and Mortal Kombat. I suck. We share a small plate of fries, mainly to soak up the alcohol. I meet my quota and it is barely 2 o'clock. Leaving Dave and Busters, I hop in Mike's truck and we go to a driving range. I know nothing about golf, but I'm going with the flow of his plan. We hit a few balls, we sit inside with more drinks for Mike, and we talk for a couple of hours. He asks if I'm hungry for real food and I nod yes.

This is by far the longest date I've ever been on. Throughout the day we chat about everything from our childhoods to future aspirations. He shares that he was married before for five years and that he's a shy and emotional guy. He says that it took him a long while to be ok with those facets of his being. This caused me to think about my representative. Surprisingly, she hadn't shown up today.

I then had, an epiphany. The authentic me can no longer only be reserved for close friends and family. Where's the freedom in that? I recognized that while walking fully in my own being on this date that there's a freedom that lives in this space that I had not felt before. I smile at the thought of what it would be like to have a partner really *know* me.

Mike seems to study me because he asked, "What are you smiling about?"

Moment of truth ... *do I share my actual thought or do I make up something else?* In what would be my first encounter with choosing to be authentic, I share, "Authenticity"

"Authenticity? What do you mean?"

"Would you agree that sometimes when meeting new people, you put your best foot forward?" I asked.

"I suppose," Mike answers. It sounds like more of a question than a statement.

"Well, I feel that the whole 'best foot forward' is our representative. It's the best parts of who we are being presented. Kinda like advertisement to get a person interested and coming back for more. But I don't think that is always a lasting thing. It's like presenting near perfection. A trap."

Mike looks intently and I don't know how to interpret that so I continue.

"But," I say louder, "If we just strive to be true, genuine and authentic, then the person we are interacting with can make a more informed decision and if we pique their interest, that too is genuine."

"Ok, I think I follow you. So, what do you think prevents people from showing up fully as their true selves in the first place?"

I like his question and avert my eyes, "Fear."

"Fear?"

"Yes. Fear of being judged, rejected, unapproved of. So rather than seeing the so called rejection as an early dismissal, we internalize that to mean that something must be wrong with us. So the representative shows up and can ultimately take over, causing inauthenticity."

"Interesting," I could tell he was processing this concept deeply.

"May I admit something?"

"Of course" Mike leans closer.

"In the spirit of transparency, I don't feel like my representative needs to make an appearance with you."

He smiles, "Is that so?"

"Yes. That is so."

"Why do you think that is."

Hmmm. "I'd say that it's because I feel safe enough to show up as myself. No need for that level of protection."

"That's interesting and I appreciate you. If your representative is better than what I've seen today, then I'd be sold out ... quick."

I laugh, "But that's not a sustainable version of me. Representatives aren't long lasting."

"Touché"

A pivotal moment in time. I believe that we are both surprised by our levels of transparency. I am drawn to him like a magnet and he to me. It is obvious. The eye contact and subtle touches are evidence that something otherworldly is happening here. This is intoxicating. Being in Mike's presence, sharing private details that had been reserved only for our own minds, experiencing a level of understanding and respect for varying points of view, my goodness. This is like conversational foreplay. The mental stimulation that I crave. Then, thoughts of someone else enter my consciousness. I wonder if what I am experiencing with Mike is possible with Maurice.

Mike and I have been with each other for so long that we forget about dinner. The minute details of how we went from the driving range to dinner are a blur, but the mind blowing conversation is everything I needed.

Mike drives me back to my car in the parking lot of Dave and Busters. Two minutes down the road and he is calling. *He understands that there is an extreme connection here.* He must feel it too. Normally I would feel relieved at the mutual attraction, but this time I think, *how could he not.*

Here we are, three months in and things are going strong as ever with Mike. The connection, the conversation, the allure are all still present. We have not even been physical. We both agree that *this* time is different and we should operate as such. For both of us, in the past, we would have had sex by now and if not, at the very least some good oral. We decide to reserve that level of intimacy for a time that we both feel is right. A time not motivated by carnal attraction. We decide to commit to being intentional. The decision to not be sexual is not because we don't want to, just that we are committed to doing something that we have never done before in this experience that we have never had before. There have been a couple of times where Mike leaned in for a kiss and static electricity prevented the follow through. Being shocked on the lips hits differently than when the electrical current runs from a finger to a less sensitive body part.

This has been the most authentic I have ever been. The most vulnerable and transparent. I've come to realize that people want and claim authenticity without realizing the grit, pain, and darkness that it takes to get there. It's not a pretty road, but I have also come to realize that it is a necessary one. I feel freer with Mike and myself.

Tonight, he's cooking dinner for me and says that he has something that he wants to share. He has let me know he's also on-call with his job, so this dinner date might be shorter than normal. Normal for us has typically been 3-4 hours of time. I plan to run home following an appointment, shower, and head his way. Time is of the essence as I want as much time with him as possible, which is nothing new. I arrive at his place at exactly 8pm. The house smells delicious.

He greets me with a sweet red wine. "Hey beautiful. Just a few moments, the main course is complete and I am putting the finishing touches on our salads."

I am amazed by what I see as I approach the table. My plate contains a fried lobster tail topped with three scallops, homemade loaded potatoes au gratin, a side salad with what Mike describes as a lemon sugar cane dressing and a slice of buttered French bread. He told me that he could cook, but damn.

His plate is loaded with a T-bone steak instead of lobster and the same accompaniments. There is soft jazz playing in the background and the lights are down low. This date is like we're in a private romantic restaurant. We sit at the table to enjoy our dinner and of course the discussion commences about how he learned to cook this way. "My brother attended culinary school before becoming an engineer. He would come home and show the family everything he learned. I had an inquisitive mind and picked up every ounce of what my brother shared."

"Wow. That's amazing."

"So pair the second hand knowledge with doing my own research, a little trial and error, I make a pretty decent home chef."

God is there anything this man can't do.

I had eaten all that I could stand without being overly stuffed, Mike clears my plate, and asks from the kitchen, "Would you like a dessert wine with your dessert?"

I admit that I have never had dessert wine. Another moment of transparency that my representative would have historically shown up to quell. I ask for water instead, which he brought out with a plate of small sweet treats. There is a rose shaped apple puff with caramel drizzle, puffed cups filled with pudding, and what looks to be fruit filled flaky egg rolls.

Impressed yet again, I ask, "What's the occasion?"

Mike takes a deep breath, "I want to take our relationship to the next level." He looks nervous. "I understand that we both have a past that has left us scarred and bruised, but I want to help you heal all that. I want you to be my lady."

I immediately want to say yes, but undoubtedly there is hesitation. I don't want to jump the gun. After all, Maurice is still in the picture, even if in a smaller capacity, he is still present.

There is such innocence in his request. His intentionality is superb. He makes it a point to leave nothing to my imagination with regards to his feelings and desires for me. The hesitation is undeniable, at least for me.

I divert his attention with a kiss, but no answer to his question. Just a soft and deliberate kiss. He is slow and methodical as if to taste the sweetness he just served me. I have had passionate kisses before, but there is something different about Mike's kisses. His desire is evident while giving short pecks that lead to longer open mouth kisses while also caressing my back, my face, and holding my hands. Again my mind goes to Maurice. The phone rings. He isn't swift to answer, but knowing that he is on-call, he must. And indeed, he is being called in to work. He has two hours to get there.

He returns to my lips as if he has no place else to be. I grab his face and the passion deepens. Clothes are tugged and removed and before I know it, in the middle if Mike's living room, he is naked and I am in my intimates. He takes a step back and looks at me. He sees me. His smile lets me know that he indeed likes what he sees.

He takes my hand and leads me to his bedroom. He lays me on the bed, and standing over me, caresses my legs. He retreats to light candles and turns off the recessed lighting. He returns to my lips, lightly kissing and licking. A slight nibble on my neck sends waves of pleasure through my entire body. He unfastens my bra with one hand while the other strokes my hair. He looks in my eyes as if he can see my soul.

Mike tickles my body with his hands, lips, and tongue with great familiarity, as if he's been here before. His teeth glide my panties from my hips. My legs open automatically and Mike accepts the invitation. He snacks on my wet spot softly and like a professional. He's careful and calculated.

He stimulates my breast with one hand and inserts two fingers of the other inside of me. I moan with delight. The wave of ecstasy washes over me, leaving my fingertips and toes tingling. My leg jerks as I try to maintain my composure. Just as I try to catch my breath from one orgasm, Mike pushes his thick manhood inside of me gently and slowly. He looks me deep in my eyes as he does so. It's like he wants to see my reaction to the first time his thickness invades my wetness.

He returns to kissing me and touching my body while slowly pushing himself inside of me. He rising again to look me in the eyes. Now it's as if he is checking to make sure I'm enjoying myself. He's quiet. It's obvious that his main goal is to please. Gentle kisses; soft caresses; slow, deep strokes; pure passion. My body is on fire. My toes and fingertips tingling again, butterflies in my stomach. The space in between my legs is throbbing with moisture produced continuously. My nipples are hard and I have chill bumps all over my arms. The tiny hairs on my back and neck rise as ripples of pleasure wave through my body. I see stars, or flashes of light, I can't really tell. I can't catch my breath. I'm lost in this lustful moment on borrowed time and for a few moments time doesn't even exist.

This is tantric.

This. Is. Sinful.

In all manners if the word, sinful. The way this man makes me feel should be outlawed. My climax is like a license for him to do the same, and he is not far behind. More kisses and intense looks. No words need to be spoken.

He releases and I feel his thick penis pulsating inside of me. This experience has confirmed any suspicions about how our chemistry will translate beyond conversing.

He lays next to me holding me tightly in his arms. The occasional soft kiss on my neck. This feels like where I'm supposed to be. Mike whispers in my ear, "I have to go to work, but you are welcome to stay. I can bring you breakfast in the morning. I really like the idea of you being in my bed when I get home from work."

I agree. Mike put out a set of towels and one of his t-shirts for me. A kiss on my forehead and he retreats to shower. I don't hear him leaving. I'm fast asleep.

My physical encounters with Mike remain consistent in both frequency and action. I am thoroughly pleased on a very regular basis. I never answered the 'girlfriend' question, we just slipped into the roles of coupleship. He is very affectionate. I feel safe with him and that allows me to reciprocate the affection without concern.

Six months into whatever this is with Mike, I continue to have moments when guilt overcomes me. There is an openness between us. Things that I thought I would be judged for, he knows. Things that took me a long while to forgive myself for, he knows. Mike fully accepts me, flaws and all. Yet I haven't told him about Maurice.

The guilt is like a third party in this situation. One night, Mike finally brings up the fact that I never really agreed to being his girlfriend. I am confronted with my avoidance and lack of intentionality with defining the relationship. We both agreed to move intentionally and here I am doing the opposite. I have no words. I need time to come up with an intelligent response.

"Can we table this discussion?" I ask, because that is the only reply I could come up with. More avoidance. I needed time to process this. A therapy session would be great right about now.

The next day at work, I see Maurice standing at the door of the office building as if he were waiting for someone. I pause in my stride, but don't want to appear too obvious that my hesitation is because of him. "Good morning," I greet him first.

"Good morning beautiful," Maurice says. For the last nine months, Mike was the only one to "Good morning, beautiful," me. I smile, he grabs the door for me to enter. "Long time no see. I heard that you were working on a project and temporarily changed your schedule."

"Yeah, I did." *Who the hell told him that?* "It was so involved that I needed a vacation after it," I offered more than what was needed.

"I've missed seeing you. How was your vacay?"

"It was nice. Not long enough at all."

"I get that. Well, can I take you to lunch today? I'd like to catch up."

For some reason I feel unable to say no. Rather than my representative taking the lead, guilt is now in the driver's seat. I agree to have lunch with Maurice.

"Cool. Can we meet here in the lobby at 11 a.m.?"

"Sure, see you then." I hop on the elevator to escape.

I enter my office, heart pounding replaying the entire interaction with Maurice wondering why on Earth I agreed to have lunch with him. *I'll take this as an opportunity to tell him about Mike.* I call my assistant Sloane to my office.

"Yes ma'am?"

"Sloane, I have a non-work-related question for you. To get your opinion on something."

"Yes ma'am. Ask away," Sloane agrees in her cheerful tone.

"What constitutes cheating in a relationship?"

Sloane looks at me with bulging eyes as if she wants to call me a slut-puppy. I can see in her expression that she wants to ask follow up questions before answering. She doesn't, "Uh. I-I would say doing anything that you wouldn't want your partner to do or even know that you did."

She has a good answer. *No a great answer.* "Thank you."

"Yes ma'am."

Sloane didn't tell me anything that I didn't already know. If the shoe were on the other foot, I would be highly pissed off if Mike agreed to go to lunch with another woman. I pick up my phone to call to cancel the lunch date, but get distracted by my cell phone's text alert. It's Mike telling me that he made reservations for dinner tonight if I was cool to go.

GUILT.

Even in the mist of us being on shaky ground, he is looking out for me. We have a standing commitment to date night and he is still willing to honor that. I respond by texting back, "yes, I want to go." I slip into a daydream about what dinner tonight would be like. I know I need to put my shit to the side and work to get over this little rough patch. Come clean about Maurice and admit to why I'm being evasive about our relationship status.

In this moment I realize that I have deep feelings for Mike that I had not conveyed verbally. I hoped that he could tell that I care deeply for him with my actions, but I understand that isn't the same as verbalizing it. I spend the better part of the morning thinking about

Mike. Between getting lost in my thoughts and actually doing some work, I did not cancelled lunch with Maurice. In all honesty, there is a part of me that doesn't want to cancel. The same part that prevents me from agreeing to identifying what Mike and I are doing as a relationship.

"Ms. Tab, you have a call on the line, should I buzz him through?" Sloane interrupts my thoughts.

"Who is it, Sloane?"

"Oh sorry. It's Dr. Jones."

Maybe Maurice was calling to cancel on me. Nerves are now balled up in the pit of my stomach.

"Yes, please buzz him through." The phone beeps twice. "This is Tabitha," I answered.

"Hey pretty lady, we still on for lunch?" Maurice asks.

I should decline and tell him about Mike and that I can't interact with him like that anymore. I don't.

"Yes. I'll be right down. Are you driving?"

"I am. See you soon."

"Yep." *Damn Tab, what's wrong with you. Tell him about Mike at lunch.*

Maurice takes me to the dive bar with the great tacos that I love. It's hard to resist these tacos. We order carne asada street tacos, margaritas, and split Tres Leches cake.

This looks like a date. Hell it feels like a date. This could be considered cheating by Sloane's definition.

I tried to ease my mind by reminding myself that I'm technically not in a relationship. That is also the exact reason why Mike and I needed to have a conversation. We made it through the entire meal and I made no mention of Mike. Maurice and I talk about vacations and work. We share about upcoming holiday plans. And still nowhere did I slide in there, *hey, I have been seeing someone else.* Once again, I'm all in my head. Looking over my shoulder because I was in fact doing something I would be pissed about if it were done to me.

"Tabitha, I've missed you," Maurice says breaking through my thoughts. His admission caught me off guard. "I know we didn't really have a chance to nurture our connection, but I do feel there is something between us and I'd like to explore that."

THIS IS THE PERFECT TIME, TABITHA. I smile and nod anticipating more from him. I like the idea of Maurice now sharing his thoughts and feelings. All I offer is a calm smile.

"Uh, I liked kissing you. I enjoyed being with you. Is that something we can get back to?" Maurice asks with such sincerity while reaching for my hand.

I've got to say something. This can't continue. *Fuck!*

"Oh Maurice. I'm flattered and I really did enjoy you too, but I'm seeing someone now." It pains me to tell him that after he shared a piece of his soul. This has to be hard to hear for a man like Maurice. For a moment I feel stupid. Here I sit across from this sweet caramel man with a silky smooth deep voice admitting to wanting me. The very man who I know for a fact checks off most of the boxes of my own "Ideal Man" list, is proclaiming his interest in me and I shoot him down. I grab his hand in an attempt to soften the words I just spoke. "Maurice, you're a great guy. I just didn't think you wanted anything more."

I can see the disappointment in his eyes as he looks up at me, "And you said you didn't want anything serious. That you didn't want a relationship. I thought we were on the same page. Then when I realized that I was really developing stronger feelings for you, I figured I better say something. Too little, too late, huh."

Fuck! "Well a-at that time, I thought that we had an understanding. I figured we were just moving slow. I accepted that, but there were no follow up conversations about what we were doing or where this was going, so I figured you were cool not progressing." *Fuck!*

"I get it. I waited too late to shoot my shot."

"I'm sorry," I manage while feeling like shit. *If only he had told me this months ago.*

"No Tab, no need to apologize," He said with a smirk, "I'll be buzzing around waiting for him to fuck up."

"What?"

Maurice boldly repeats himself, "I'll continue to apply pressure in hopes that whomever you are choosing will fuck up. I mean, I won't be disrespectful, but you know ... I feel what I feel."

I didn't expect this response. *Is this dude basically saying fuck the dude you're seeing?* The waitress delivers the ticket. Maurice pulls out his American Express and slides it in the folder, never breaking eye contact with me. He is dead ass serious. I'm speechless.

"I mean, I won't disrespect your situation, but I will be paying attention. When I was a teen, I overheard my father giving my oldest brother relationship advice. It was bad advice for my brother's situation seeing as how he was caught cheating on his girlfriend, but he said something that I never forgot. 'You're single till you're married, son' is what my father told my brother."

"Ok wait. So your brother was caught cheating and your father justified it by saying 'You're single till you're married'?"

Maurice laughed, "Yep. I told you it was terrible advice for his situation, but nevertheless, I think it applies here. Tabitha, you're single till you're married, babe. Again, I won't be disrespectful, but I will be paying attention."

"Maurice what if the shoe were on the other foot?" *He can't be serious.*

"I wouldn't fuck up. There would be no room for another man to slip in."

Damn. The level of cockiness. I nod. That's all I've got, a slow nod.

Well this didn't go as I thought it would. Maurice's reaction and response are definitely unexpected. In a twisted way, I've never felt more desired.

We ride back to work in silence. Me still trying to wrap my head around this entire lunch and Maurice with a satisfied smirk on his face. We arrive and enter the building, still no words spoken. We enter the elevator and press the numbers of our respective floors, still no words. We ascend and reach Maurice's floor first. He reaches down, grabs my hand and squeezed, still no words. He walks off the elevator and I ascend higher, completely dumbfounded.

Date night with Mike is at a restaurant that resembles a place we visited on one of our out of state adventures. It's a blend of lounge and upscale dining. Reservations are a must because this place has been hopping since opening two months ago. That's about how long it took us to get in.

There is a DJ playing music from my favorite era. We walk in to Deborah Cox repeatedly asking, *How did you get here?* There was a time that this song resonated so greatly with me. Today, I simply enjoy it and sing along without the emotional attachment. It's already a nice vibe. The energy is high and people appear to be in their own worlds, completely engrossed in whatever is happening at their tables. We are seated in the middle of the restaurant, but against the wall in a semi-circle booth.

After sliding to the middle of the booth, I look up at Mike. He has the most sincere and endearing look about him. I take in all of him. His bright eyes, his perfect lips framed by a well maintained beard and mustache, his bald head, they all do it for me. I smile. He gives a half smile. There is an awkwardness between us because we have been in disagreement and then there is Maurice, a factor unbeknownst to Mike.

Mike smiles, "I've missed you. Baby, I'm sorry that my communication with you has been missing the mark lately. I don't quite know how to fix it completely, but I need you to know that I am all in. Tabitha, I love you and I have realized these last couple of weeks just how much I need you in my life."

Wow. This admission is unexpected. I admit that I miss the connection too and apologize for the confusion I have caused.

The waitress approached the table for our drink orders. At the exact same time that I look up to answer her, I see Maurice walking by with two other guys. He makes eye contact with me so strong that I feel the urgent need to look away. *What in the entire fuck?* The guilt is back.

"Babe," Mike asks interrupting my thoughts.

"Yes?"

"What are you drinking?"

"Oh, uh, I'll take a Lemon Drop."

"Oooh excellent choice," the waitress replies. "Our martinis are amazing and I'm sure you will love them. The Lemon Drop is infused with lemon oil and the rim is piled with brown cane sugar. It's a top pick."

I am impressed by her description. "What did you order hun?" I ask Mike.

I was so thrown off by Maurice walking past our table that I completely missed his selection.

"An Old Fashioned."

"Another great choice," the waitress chimes in.

"Are there any bad choices?" I ask.

"Actually there are some drinks on the menu that I'm not fond of, but for the most part, our mixologists are great at what they do. They each have incorporated their own flavor into classic drinks such as the martinis, Old Fashioned, Long Island Ice Tea, and the margaritas," she says with a smile.

I like how she took the time to offer more insight. Her answer is also a good transition from my utter shock of seeing Maurice to bringing me back to my date. The person who should have my attention.

"Take your time looking over the menu. If you would like suggestions, please let me know. I would be happy to help you decide. I'll be back shortly with your drinks."

The DJ is now playing a mix of Mtume's "Juicy Fruit", "The One" by Tamar Braxton, and "Juicy" by Notorious B.I.G. I love it.

"You want some hookah?" Mike asks while laughing.

"Uh no, I'm cool on hookah for a while," I can tell that he thought of our first meeting and how horrible I was at smoking hookah that night. I'm glad he still finds it amusing. It definitely keeps me humble.

Mike laughs more and says, "I thought your attempt was cute. It's what attracted me to you. I like that someone I view as perfect for me, could show imperfections with grace."

I love the compliment. "So you want me to smoke to show you how imperfect I am?" I ask for clarification, but mainly to keep the conversation going. He has no idea the depth of my imperfections.

"Not exactly. I'm offering the smoke because I love to see you try. What I have come to know about you is that your 'go getter' attitude won't allow you *not* to try. That goes for anything. You trying to smoke hookah lets me see that. And ... I think it would lighten the mood we have been in."

I can see his point, but can think of a few ways to lighten the mood without me getting choked up on smoke. The music is one way, people are now bopping to the sounds of BBD's "Poison".

I decide to be transparent for a moment to see if that helps, "Mike I want you to know that I feel that I don't see the need to rush into a commitment at the moment. I've missed our seamless connection and I want to get back to that. Just being here with you lightens the energy between us for me. The music helps and I'm sure the drinks will further help the situation. I think sometimes we just have to decide to move on. In my opinion the original issue is null and void, but the way we communicated about it is where the issue lies. The faulty communication gets addressed by us communicating better and making good attempts to do so."

"I understand and respect that."

We both smile and welcome our waitress back. I can remain noncommittal for a little while longer. She places our drinks before us and I must say, they look top shelf in presentation alone. Mine topped heavily with the brown cane sugar and a spiral of lemon peel. Mike's with a large round cube of ice with what looks to be a leaf of basil frozen inside of it. Atop the drink is a shaved piece of orange peel. The presentation is superb.

"Are you beautiful people ready to order?"

Mike orders for us both, "Yes ma'am. The lady will have the salmon, risotto, and a Caesar salad and I'll have the top sirloin, twice baked potatoes and asparagus."

"Excellent choices, how would you like your steak, sir?"

"Medium, please"

As our amazing waitress finishes up with Mike, my attention is pulled away by the buzz of my cell phone. I look down to see a text from Maurice, *"You look really nice this evening!"*

Out of habit, I look around to see where he is and spot him almost immediately. He is ironically seated across the aisle from us, two tables away and his particular seat placement puts him behind Mike with a clear shot at me. *This is some stalker type shit.*

"You ok, babe?" Mike asks reaching his hand to me atop the table.

I am brought back to where I am supposed to be and notice that the waitress has left.

"Yes, hun. I'm fine."

"I meant to tell you that you look really nice this evening," Mike flirts with me.

Fuck my life. The exact same words?

"Thank you baby. You aren't too shabby yourself," I flirt back. Mike scoots over to get closer to me. He leans in to give me a kiss on the lips.

I don't close my eyes because I am peeking behind him to see if Maurice is looking. He is. *Damn. This is weird.*

"What you got on under all this?" Mike asks pulling at my skirt.

I had to look down to remind myself of the outfit I had on. Red, A-line, pleated, mid-calf skirt, black lace top and black stilettos. I did look damn good. Underneath, I had on a black lace bra and a pair of black lace thongs. The overlapping lace prevents my nipples from showing. Enough is revealed to make a man's mouth water, but enough is concealed to require him to use his imagination.

One of the things that I love most about Mike is that he is secure. He isn't bothered by the clothing I wear because he knows I'm with him and that no matter how sexy my outfit is, it will first and foremost be classy.

I whisper in his ear the description of my undergarments. While doing so, I allow my lips to lightly brush up against his ear and make sure to magnify my breathing. I touch his leg under the table. Starting at the knee, I move slowly up and feel that his manhood has swollen under his fitted slacks. With my lips still lightly touching his ear, I glance up and see Maurice looking directly at me. I whisper, "Can I take you home with me tonight?"

"Hell yeah," Mike responds. He now has his hand under my skirt caressing my thighs.

"I can tell you have something nasty on your mind," I continue to whisper in his ear.

"I do. It's called make up sex."

"Mmmm," I moan in Mike's ear.

The DJ started to play a slow jam type vibe. *I Get Lonely* by Janet Jackson begins its melodic intro. I recognize it instantly. Lifting my head to look at Mike's face, his eyes still closed and he is biting his bottom lip, we are definitely on our own world with a peeping Tom across the way. Mike takes a sip of his drink. I do the same.

"You want another?" he asks.

"Oh no, this thing is loaded with vodka. It's smooth and all and taste really good, but another would have me on my ass."

Mike waves to our waitress and she hurries over.

"Babe, I don't want nor need another drink," I plead.

"I need you to have another though."

"But why?"

"I want to do some nasty shit to you this evening and I need you wide ass open."

I laugh, "Mike, you should know by now that I don't need alcohol to get nasty. Especially nasty with you."

I pull his arm to lower him to me so that I can whisper in his ear again. I get close enough for my lips to resume their position on his ear.

"Yes, sir?" our waitress asks.

Mike clears his throat, still lowered to my mouth, "May we have more water?"

"Absolutely," and as quickly as she arrived, she is gone.

I whisper, "Baby, you don't need to liquor me up to do nasty shit to or with me. You can do whatever you like, whenever you like, however you like."

Mike turns to me to look me in the eyes, "How did I get so lucky?"

"Intentionality baby. Being in the right place at the right time, and being clear about what you want."

Dinner is fabulous and we know we will be back. As we walk out of the restaurant, I look at the table where Maurice had been sitting and notice that he and his party had already departed. I am slightly relieved that I don't have to walk past him on our way out.

We step outside and Mike hands the ticket to the valet to retrieve his car. My phone buzzes with a text message. I look down to see that it's Maurice again.

DAMN!!!! I don't check the message.

I look to my left and see him standing just a few yards from me. He looks me up and down and with a furrowed brow, nods his head as if to approve.

I mouth the word *"STOP"* and he smiles. Just then the car is parked in front of us. Mike walks me to the passenger side, opens my door. He makes sure that I and all of my skirt are securely inside before shutting the door and walking to the driver's side. He tips the valet and we leave.

It is a magical weekend with Mike at my house until that Sunday night. We made up all weekend long. We ordered in and did not leave once we were safely behind my door on Friday after dinner. Our phones were off and we watched Netflix all weekend long. We remained in PJs and fashion socks and lounged on the couch for much of the weekend, except for sleeping and sexing in the bed.

I didn't want to return to work on Monday. Mainly because I didn't want to leave Mike's arms, but also because I didn't want to face Maurice. I arrive earlier than normal thinking that I could avoid him that way. It doesn't work. He is at the coffee counter in the lobby as I walk in the door. It's as if he's waiting on me.

He made no hesitation on his way to me, "Good morning beautiful."

"Good morning Maurice."

"Can I get you a coffee?"

"No thank you. I had coffee at home this morning."

Maurice nods and begins, "Hey, I want apologize for interrupting your date with my texts. It looked like you guys were really enjoying yourselves."

"We were and thanks for the apology."

"May I ask one thing, Tabitha?"

Oh shit. I stop and lower my bag in irritation, "Sure."

Maurice pulls his lips in and rubs his goatee. For a moment I looked at his lips as if I miss them. As if I want to taste the traces of coffee on them. A smirk appears and I realize immediately that he can see me looking and lusting for his lips. "Tabitha, did you enjoy me when we spent time together outside of work?"

What the fuck. A sigh escapes me, "Maurice why are you asking this?"

"I just want to know. I think about you often and wonder if the enjoyment was mutual."

Reluctantly I answer, "Yes, Maurice. I did enjoy you."

"So what happened, lady? I've been wracking my brain trying to figure out how I went from the guy you were chilling with to you kicking it with someone new totally with no warning."

I suppose on some level I owe him an explanation. I consider that if what I did by ignoring the situation with Maurice were done to me, I would be hurt and pissed. "Maurice, I did like you. Uh, I-I do like you. I did enjoy the time with you and the things we did, but I started to want more than you seemed to want to give. That allowed room for someone who wanted what I wanted to come in and ..." I stop. I should have left it there, but in my attempt to soften the blow I add, "I miss you sometimes and seeing you here on the regular makes things difficult."

"Difficult how?"

He's pulling me in and I can't believe that I am stepping in this shit. "It's difficult to see you and remember the things you did to my body and not allow any of that to continue."

He smiled.

FUCK! I need to shut up. I've said too much.

"I can still give it to you and it would be our little secret."

A whole ass inappropriate proposition, "Duly noted." *Close the motherfuckin' door Tab!*

Maurice continues, "If you had told me that your position had changed, you know given me the opportunity to let you know that I wanted more as well, maybe things would be different."

I give a half smile, lower my head and rush to catch the open elevator as two people ease off. I nearly knock one of them down trying like hell to get away from Maurice. I look at him as the doors close. He has a look of satisfaction on his face. As if he feels that he still has a chance.

Lesson 16: Therapy

I sit on Dr. Drea's couch twirling my fingers. It's not often that I initiate the silence that sometimes fills this space. She allows it. A good eight minutes pass with no words spoken. It's like we are waiting each other out. I'll lose because Dr. Drea has great patience and patience is not my strong suit.

Breaking the silence I ask, "I've been coming to see you for about a year now. How am I not better at this whole love and relationship thing? How have I not figured this part of life out yet? I resolve that I completely suck at relationships. I legit don't know what to do or how to do it."

Dr. Drea continues the silence for a bit longer. She takes a sip of her tea before saying, "Perhaps you have gotten better, are better and have a few things figured out, but right at this juncture, you are just now attempting to connect it all. Have you considered that maybe the lessons you have been remembering weren't as evident to you because you hadn't really needed to lean on them until now? Tabitha, we don't ever stop learning. Our education on life doesn't cease once we have accomplished many of our goals. Experiences continue to happen. Life moves along. Lessons continue to be learned. Having an outlet and trusted support system for which you can process all of this is key. *This* is what you haven't had before until the last year. Maybe that's the difference."

Dr. Drea always offers a great alternate perspective, and I love her for it.

I say nothing. I wait for her to continue. Maybe the answer to what I should do is coming up next. I don't know why I find comfort in someone else making the tough decisions for me. I don't know where that came from or why that still rings true, because it never works out well. Relinquishing my power for someone else to decide things for me never ends the way I want it to or the way I need it to for that matter. Dr. Drea for the first time ever, breaks the silence. I won. I beat her at the silent treatment.

"Tabitha, what evidence do you have that speaks to the notion that you 'suck at relationships'? Last I heard, you and Mike were doing well."

I take a moment, "My situation with Mike is going like most relationships go. It ebbs and flows. We aren't perfect people and do not have a perfect relationship. I think I can confidently speak for him when I say that we aren't aiming for perfection. We want longevity. A lasting love that cuts through any adversity that may come our way. It just so happens that my adversity is Maurice."

Dr. Drea cuts in, "May I ask a question frankly?"

Aw shit, Dr. Drea is about to cut me. She always prefaces her hard knocks by asking for permission. It's like Mike Tyson asking if he can punch you in the face. Who the fuck would say yes to that? Me. I say yes to a question from Dr. Drea that will be the equivalent to being punched in the face by Mike Tyson. A Tyson in his prime type punch at that.

"If the goal for your relationship with Mike is long lasting love that isn't perfect, what role does Maurice play in that? How is he your adversity?"

TKO. *Damn.* I knew it would be a hell of a question, but I'm not prepared for this yet. I suppose in examining what's wrong with Mike and me, I do need to address the elephant in the situation. "Mike and I have had a rough month and I didn't exactly agree to be his girlfriend, we've just assumed the positions. Maurice is a distraction. It's like I fear Mike will let me down, like he'll tell me that he doesn't want this. That he doesn't want me. Like, I will wake up one day and he will just be gone from my life. It's like ... like I'm preparing myself for the heartbreak. On some level, I see Maurice as my safety net." I take a breath to gather my thoughts before continuing, "Maurice has expressed continued interest. I love the feeling of being *this* desired. I haven't told Mike about Maurice. I just recently told Maurice about Mike."

"And Maurice is there to catch you when or if your situation with Mike fails?"

"I don't know Dr. Drea."

"Oh Tabitha, remember this is a no 'I don't know' zone. That phrase is reserved for when we don't want to think. Here we think and talk things through."

Ugh. I know this is why I come to therapy, but this is hard. "I suppose Maurice is there to catch me, should Mike kick me to the curb or ghosts me. Maybe on some level I am sabotaging things with Mike as a means of having some type of control." My eyes find the amethyst box. It sits on my left instead of the coffee table that I'm used to seeing it. "It's easy for me to just leave. Leave before I get left. Maybe that's my toxic trait. This is how my abandonment trauma is showing up. My protective shield or a trauma response. At the first sign of trouble or discord, I want to bail. When you've been abandoned as much as I feel that I have been, you try to maintain the upper hand in how the relationship unfolds, especially if it is headed to an ending. It's like a power trip. For some odd reason, I find that ending things on my terms brings me comfort. It's better than the unknown."

"May I be frank again?"

Aw shit. Here comes the two of that one, two knockout punch, "Of course Doc."

"Does that make sense to you when you hear it aloud? Like do you even hear yourself?"

These must be rhetorical questions because Dr. Drea continues to speak frankly.

"So you're saying that you would much rather abandon the relationship or refuse to define things so that you can do the dumping instead of being dumped when there is no indication that Mike wants to discontinue the relationship? Do you really feel that your relationship is in jeopardy to that degree? Have you spoken to Mike about your feelings?"

More rhetorical questions, and she keeps going. This is her way of making me think deeper.

"You'd rather break your own heart than work your shit out? Is that what you really want? Is Maurice what you want?"

Ooooh! My stupidity broke Dr. Drea. She's never read me for filth in this manner before.

"Tabitha, seriously, what do you want?"

That last question isn't rhetorical. The previous questions are to shake the shit out of me so that I can answer the real question with a semblance of intellect. So if the answer *I don't know* is unacceptable, I better get to thinking. I better also get to confessing. Dr. Drea doesn't have the entire story.

Examining the amethyst box out of place on the side table, I gather my thoughts. "Ok, so here goes ... I have allowed the door to stay open for Maurice because I don't consistently feel secure in this thing with Mike. When we disagree, I equate that to him getting fed up with my shit and wanting to leave." Emotion begins to well. *Keep it together and continue*, I think. "From my past experiences, dealing with that level of rejection was hard as shit. Maurice is my safety net, so to speak, to lessen the blow of being left. Of being alone. To answer your questions honestly, I want them both. I find comfort in having them both in my life. I don't want to choose. I know that my rationale at this point makes no sense and is utter, selfish bullshit. I like Maurice and see his value. I didn't fully give him a chance, so it's like he's too good to let go.

I understand that I would have the same issues with him because *I am* the issue. I do think that I am catastrophizing things with Mike because I just don't know how to navigate a mature, serious relationship."

Dr. Drea listens intently. My eyes burn from tears ready to fall.

"Of all the love lessons I have recalled with you, none of them were lasting relationships. I still don't know how to do that and it scares me. Not knowing what to do or how to do it, terrifies me." My nose is burning from trying to suppress emotions that need to come out. Dr. Drea allows me silence. "None of this is fair to Maurice or Mike, and I get that. I have left the door open for Maurice, conversing with him and allowing him to cross a boundary. The man told me that he's fallen in love with me. How did I end up in a love triangle?" That was my rhetorical question because I know exactly how I got here.

"Tabitha, can you tell why you really left the door open? Is it more than having a safety net?"

I sit twiddling my fingers and staring at the pretty box. The tears start to flow freely now. It's a quiet cry, but I don't wipe the tears because they are flowing so fast. I finally answer, "Yes. It's more than having a safety net for a relationship that isn't crumbling the way I present it to be. I like the attention of a man of Maurice's stature. A part of me feels that I didn't give him the attention or time for things to develop into something more. He ... he fits a certain aesthetic."

"And why is that important to you, Tabitha?"

"Because my history is that I have either settled, been left, or was looked over and for once, I can choose. On some level I don't want to choose. I want to experience the idea of having options a little longer."

"But at what cost, Tabitha?" Dr. Drea asks softly as if it pained her to ask the question.

Damn! At what cost, I repeat her question in my mind. In the end, it is inevitable that one of us will be hurt. I have to look beyond myself and make a choice. It's not all about self-preservation. I am potentially holding up the healing of a great man because I want to feel wanted and desired for a little while longer. The price is high no matter the choice, but it doesn't have to be self-sacrificial.

"Have you been intimate with both men?"

"Oh no, ma'am. I am only intimate with Mike. Maurice isn't getting that part of me. He's getting way too much of my attention and time, but we have not been physically intimate since that time in his office. Before Mike."

"So he has your mind ... your attention?"

Catch-22, both options are terrible and one leads to the other. I nod. "We speak on a regular basis and I have gone to lunch with him a few times. Since I've been seeing Mike, we have kissed and if there were less restraint, I'm sure it would have gone further. For some reason, I feel that we have spoken more deeply and openly through all of this."

"What do you want, Tabitha?"

That question again. "I want to be with one man. One good man. I want him to have all of me as I want to have all of him. I need to feel safe and secure."

"Is your insecurity concerning Mike something that he can help alleviate?"

"I honestly don't think so. He can offer all the reassurance in the world, but I need to work on feeling worthy of what he wants to give. The same would be true of Maurice too, I suppose."

"That's good, Tabitha. Continue."

I must have said the right thing, something full of insight. Part of Dr. Drea's therapy process is to allow me to talk and at some point I will utter the answer. She will point it out and suggest we explore it. Judging by her response, I am on the right track. I don't lack insight, I lack consistent action and follow through.

"I don't feel worthy of love from either, really." I take a deep breath, "My insecurity stems from the lessons of past situations and relationships. Situations where I was cheated on, left, or fucked up on my own, all resulting in me not getting what I wanted or needed. I didn't have enough experiences that taught me that I was valued. That I was chosen for the long haul. I try damn hard not to relive those painful experiences, but my attempts to move past them make them ever more present in my mind. It's like when one of those painful love lessons resurfaces, I think that Mike can sense it somehow and the way he interacts with me is filtered through that experience. And he has no idea about it and then there's the guilt that plagues me."

Dr. Drea writes something down. She rarely takes notes, but I said something that caught her attention enough for her to jot it down.

I continue, "That's me projecting isn't it?"

Dr. Drea nods in agreement.

I pause and return my attention to the pretty box. With a sharp inhale I continue, "If my attention wasn't divided, no matter the fractional delegation, I could effectively attend to the adversities that arise in my relationship. Maurice is doing what men do. They allow a good woman to slip through their fingers, and when she moves on, they look for a sliver of light that they can use to ease back in. I chose not to push the door shut. There was a small opening that he pushed and I allowed to open wider. So now I have two good men professing their love for me. I'm not gonna lie Doc, this shit feels good to be so desired, but at the same time, it's eating me alive from the inside. My conscious is all jacked up. I'm all over the place. I feel guilty so I create problems where none exist so that Mike could get mad at me, enough to leave me. That's what I deserve, to be discarded for playing with his emotions. It's not what I want by any means, but if that were to happen, I couldn't be mad." I took a breath and sat with all I said for a moment. I'm using therapeutic silence now.

Dr. Drea allowed me that time before speaking, "See you do get it, Tabitha. Sometimes, you just need a safe space to speak your truth without judgement or consequence. To get all the junk out of your head without concern for how it may sound to someone else. Once we acknowledge things, we can begin to heal them." She smiles a warm smile in my direction and then jots a few more things in her planner. She continues, "So what's next?"

I am exhausted, but I feel lighter. "Ooooh, take it slow Doc," I say. We both laugh.

"I mean in terms of your next move towards walking in honesty."

Oh. Shit, I don't know! "Uh. I- I suppose I need to figure out which one I want to be with."

"Is that a tough decision for you?"

"The tough part is knowing that I will hurt someone and have to live with that. That I will have to share completely what's been going on with me and be willing to accept the response. The idea of all of that breaks my heart because neither of these men deserve that. I realize that I have strong feelings for them both. I hadn't admitted that aloud. I need to sit with that too."

"What do you think your process will be? Have you considered going back to the beach for a weekend? When you went last time, you returned with such clarity."

Dr. Drea made a good point and I can add that to the list of things I consider. "I do agree that stepping away from it all can be helpful. Maybe I will do that. It will almost bring this entire process full circle."

"Yes, in a way I can see that. Do you see the growth since you last went to the beach?"

I giggle, "I suppose there has been some growth, but there has also been new fuckery." I think back over what has occurred since my last trip to paradise. I take a quick, bittersweet walk down memory lane that produces a few tears and a smile or two. I met and entertained three dudes in a matter of months, two of which still linger resulting in a damn love triangle. "It's been an interesting road, to say the least."

"Good, so you'll go? Should we schedule for after you return to discuss that process and your decision?'

"I like the idea of that and will call to schedule after I have finalized my plans and will know when I will return. Dr. Drea, I thank you for everything. Your realness was most definitely needed."

"No need to thank me Tabitha. Just remember focus more on what you need and want and focus less on pleasing others."

"Yes ma'am."

What I love most about Friday evening sessions is that I can leave and go home and have the weekend to process my session. I sit in my car for a moment before leaving the parking lot, paralyzed by the song on the radio. Jazmine Sullivan's "Hurt Me So Good" plays and I easily drift to thoughts of toxic emotional rollercoasters and refusals to decide when it comes to romantic relationships and this song embodies so much of what I felt. I'm grateful for the realizations and the wherewithal to make changes.

On the way home, I call Sloane, "Hey Sloane, I need your help with scheduling another trip to my parent's beach house."

"Yes ma'am. When would you like to go?"

"As soon as possible. What's on my planner for this upcoming week?"

"No big cases or deals set. I'm looking at meetings noooow and you're good there too. It seems that your schedule is open for this upcoming week. Which day would you like to leave?"

Sloane is so good at her job. Think that the relaxed nature of our relationship helps her to feel at ease in her duties. How about Tuesday? That would give me Monday to set my emails and phone to out of office."

"Oh Ms. Tab, I can do that for you. It looks like the best flight options are to leave Monday and return on Saturday. How's that? Too long?"

"No Sloane, that is perfect."

Lesson 17: Tabitha

It's a whirlwind at work. I close two big deals, which, result in my consideration for a promotion. Romantically, things are about the same. Things have continued with my time being split between Mike and Maurice. I honestly don't know how I'll choose.

During my last session, I discovered that I am putting both relationships in jeopardy by allowing the door to remain open for Maurice while dating Mike and by not actually making a choice. I'm choosing to view the retreat that Dr. Drea suggested as a means to get my thoughts, feelings, and ideas together. To finally make a choice. I can surely use the time away. She gave me several journal prompts to help me process the millions of thoughts coursing through my mind at a high rate of speed. The thoughts come so fast that I can hardly keep up.

My focus on anything else has significantly diminished and I am making terrible food choices. I never considered myself an emotional eater, but this situation seriously has my entire soul vexed. The day before my session and before Sloane booked my trip, I ran into Maurice at the store between my house and the office. I hadn't seen him in a few days; at least I hadn't noticed him. He asked me out, stating that he would very much like to speak with me. We had mainly been hanging out as friends, no pressure for more.

While sharing beignets at a local coffee shop one day, Maurice had told me that he loved me. I didn't know how to respond and immediately realized that this admission greatly complicated my current situation further than was already the case.

As a result of his admission, I changed up my routine for a little while and went to great lengths to avoid running into Maurice. The thought of having a conversation with him now, especially without knowing where his head was made me uncomfortable, so I avoided it. I didn't agree to a meet up and said that I would get with him when things at work calmed down. We rarely spoke on the phone, he was much more of a face to face type guy, so avoiding him proved efficient, until today.

After my session with Dr. Drea and in preparation for my trip, I went to the office to grab a few things. I ran into Maurice in the lobby. The lobby always betrayed me.

"Hey Tab. How's it going?"

"Hey Maurice, things are good. Just stopping by to pick a few things before I head out of town." I say feeling nervous. Come to think of it, telling him that I'm headed out of town is probably too much information.

"Oh ok, well I was still hoping to chat with you for a bit. When do you think you will have time?"

"Oh Maurice, I'm not sure. Um, there is so much going on right now that I-I can't call it." *I gotta go.* I look around and continue, "I really need to head out."

He looks disappointed, "Ok, can I walk you to your car?"

"That's cool. Thanks." Such the gentleman. We walk in silence. I unlock the door and Maurice opens it for me.

"Be safe."

"I will," with a nervous smile. This feels so awkward. I'm not going to be able to avoid him much longer. Guilt's ugly presence is back. Maurice is a great guy, the time that we were spending together as "friends" reminded me of why I enjoy him so. *You gotta choose, girl!* Things have been good with Mike for the most part, aside from him being unaware of Maurice. With Mike, I barely recognize myself at times. With him, I am more open; more honest; more relaxed. It's like

I am seeing my authentic self consistently for the first time and he is the one who brought that out. I have never wanted to share every inch of my day and every ounce of my being with anyone. Maurice benefits from my newfound level of comfort which made way for a connection to reignite. So here I am with two great men professing their love for me and all I have to do is choose. I call Chaz on my drive home to make plans for her to take me to the airport for my trip.

Monday morning arrives so fast that I barely remember the weekend. I spent it alone. Mike is out of town and I didn't feel like doing anything with the girls. I spent the time packing and reflecting. I feel so heavy. My stomach in knots thinking about the gravity of my situation. *What if I choose wrong? What if my choice doesn't choose me? How serious am I ready to get? How do I feel for Mike? Maurice?* My thoughts are interrupted by a car horn. *That must be Chaz.*

"Who all knows you're running away?" Chaz asks as I jump in her car.

"I'm not running away. I am simply going to clear my mind. Clarity is a beautiful thing you know." I reply.

Chaz chuckles, "Girl call it what you want. You running!" She switches the music to a talk radio station. The men on air are in mid-sentence about inflation. Chaz scoffs and turns the radio off. "So what's this trip about anyway, since you not running?"

I've tried to keep details to a minimum, but I share, "To think deep and gain a little clarity. That is the goal, to purge old shit and discover a path to the new. Several days away from everything is plenty of time to do that."

"Mmmhmm, I guess." She replies.

I arrive at my destination ahead of schedule. The extra time affords me a moment to prepare the villa. I carefully place candles that I smuggled with me, use my sage to smudge and cleanse the space, and I make a list of things that I need to make this trip the most beneficial. The weather is nice and the bungalow is a short walk to the store. I decide to get my exercise in by making the short walk. The alcohol selections are limited to Chardonnay and Merlot. I get one of each. My plan is to journal, meditate, do some yoga and spend time in nature by way of the beach.

<JOURNAL ENTRY: JULY 9th>

It's been a wonderful getaway and soon it will be time to return home ... back to the real world. The late night rumblings of my mind bring about various emotions. Vacillating between tears from remembered pain to laughing about silly inside jokes. With my music on shuffle, I even get up to dance around to "Body Like a Back Road" by Sam Hunt and "Don't Take It Personal (Just One of Them Days)" by Monica, singing in the remote that I never used. Nearly a week of reflection led to a good amount if insight gained, deep healing and inspired vision. I've got candles going and they seem to assist with this much needed cleanse and healing that I didn't know I needed as much as I did. What seems to be the soundtrack of my life played in the background all week long and I can confidently report that I've found peace. No work, no emails, minimal calls, I can truly say that I was allowed to have my time. I realized so much. My week consisted of morning runs on the beach, brunch on the patio overlooking the ocean, journaling new thoughts and ideas and unpacking the old, adventure, and love. I sang sad love songs, danced to songs that bring me joy. I journaled some more. I cried, I napped, ate late lunches at local spots. I enjoyed drinks on the patio while watching the sun set and late take out dinners while journaling even more. At this point in my retreat, only songs of joy and love are playing because that is where I am headed! I have come to realize that love is more than an emotion. It is a choice and I have made mine.

My journaling is interrupted by a knock at the door. I seriously consider not answering because I had not ordered anything and was surely not expecting anyone. A second knock and I slowly rise from my seat on the patio to answer. Fully prepared to tell whomever was interrupting my night of peace to take a hike. *Let me get my mind right.* I open the door only to find a bouquet of flowers. An exotic blend of Birds of Paradise, Anthurium, Calla Lilies, Tulips and Protea sat at the doorstep of my villa. Simply breathtaking. There's an envelope with two notecards left with just my first name on the front. It's handwritten in a beautiful script *Tabitha*. One notecard has the #1 on it and the other has #2. I pull the bouquet in and shut the door admiring the beautiful flowers. I sit on the sofa with the beautiful bouquet. I examine each and every stem. I love fresh flowers, so I plan to enjoy these beauties while I have them. There is something about having the beauty of nature at your fingertips. My affinity for nature began at an early age. It is the reason I choose to come to the beach whenever I need to fill my cup. I easily slip into a daydream while gazing at the alluring bouquet. I lie back on the sofa and imagine the feel of the sand between my toes.

The rush of waves hitting my ankles knock me off balance even though I anticipate the crash. The breeze of fresh wind lightly spraying ocean droplets down on me cause the hairs on my arms to stand. The swooshing sound of the water and wind together soothe me as if nature herself is speaking to me and only me, I love it all! I visualize myself visiting the beach as often as I want. I see myself walking along the coastline with soft, white sand squishing between my toes. I feel the waves caressing my legs whenever my man isn't. I imagine posting up on the raised patio of my beach house at sunset writing in my journal. The man in my life bringing me a glass of red wine as I watch the sky move from a baby blue with golden streaks to the most beautiful shades of indigo. The man in my life. I like the idea of that. Sharing one of my favorite places with my man. I take a sip of my wine, he leans in to kiss me. It starts off slow and becomes deeper as low moans escape me. He tastes the cherry, black currant, and vanilla flavors left on my lips from the wine he served. This man knows a great wine. My man has no face. I can visualize everything but his face. I see his toned arms, especially his shoulders. I love strong shoulders. I can't explain why that particular body part of a man garners so much of my attention. I can visualize his strong, yet soft hands. Hands that explore my body with assurance that they are in the right place.

My phone rings. *Dammit! I can't seem to win tonight. Every time I attempt to escape in my own thoughts, I am interrupted.* This time, it's my assistant, Sloane. I realize that I am still holding one of the notecard and hadn't taken a peek inside as I answer the phone, "Hello ... is everything ok?"

"Uh, Yes ma'am. I'm just checking in with you. How are things going?" Sloane asks. There a sound of concern in her voice.

"I'm good, Sloane. You sure you're ok?" I ask again. I trace my fingers over my name written so beautifully on the notecard. I feel the raised print.

"Well ..." Sloane begins taking a deep breath before continuing, "Maurice cornered me at the office asking about you. I didn't know how to handle that, I was so caught off guard. He was telling me how he can't stop thinking about you and how he had something very important to speak with you about and how he needed to get in contact with you ASAP. He knew you were out of town and ..."

I stop Sloane. I am in complete shock. She is obviously distraught, likely thinking that she would be in some sort of trouble with me. She isn't I attempt to reassure her, "Sloane. It's ok, honey. Don't worry, it will be just fine. I did not share where I was going and my phone has been on do not disturb since I've been here. He may be a little worried. It's ok, sweetheart, I promise."

Sloane let out a deep sigh of relief.

While on the phone with her, I hear rustling sounds outside. I don't investigate because the wind has been high all day. I look down at the notecard and my intricately written name and ask, "What did you tell him?"

"I'm so sorry, Ms. Tabitha, I told him you are at your parent's beach house. I told him that you are ok and that he needn't worry." Sloane explained.

I comfort her by telling her again that things were ok. "I didn't tell anyone where I was going and I haven't been taking calls. Maurice isn't a dangerous man, he's just worried. Before I left, he said he wanted to speak with me. I didn't tell him how long I'd be gone. You didn't do a terrible thing. It'll be fine. Rest yourself and I will see you soon. It's fine I promise," I reassure.

"Yes ma'am." We hang up.

I stare at the envelope. I take a large sip of my wine before picking up my glass and walking towards the patio of my villa just as I had in my daydream. Before stepping out, I look at the notecard and decide that I would just read it out in the night breeze that seems to call for my attention. I touch the top of my head where I typically rest my glasses and they are not there. I am now in search of my glasses so that I can read the notecard without struggle. I find them in the bathroom after looking for nearly ten minutes.

I step out of the villa onto the patio, surprised to see candles flickering on the table, the railing and even the steps leading to the beach. I take a step back inside so that I am not exposed. I peek out to the left and the right and begin again out onto the patio. Easing out of the sliding glass door, I see that more flowers adorn the small table. My eyes move from left to right taking in all that is before me. I am in complete shock and for a moment, I can't discern if I am really seeing such staging or if the large gulp of wine caused me to slip back into Fantasyland without me realizing it.

I step further onto the patio and soft music begins to play as if on cue. It's a beautiful melody that I hadn't heard before. It seems to fit the scene perfectly and blends very well with the sounds of waves crashing ashore. I look around and see no one. Thanks to the night breeze, I catch a very pleasing scent that is familiar to me. The palm trees on both sides of the patio are rustling softly in the breeze. The trees could easily explain the sound I heard from inside the house, but someone is here.

The scent catches my attention again as the breeze picks up. I can't recall the scent and no particular memory comes to mind, but I do feel a familiar rush of good vibes. I look to my right and see a single red rose with a folded notecard attached. My name written in the same gorgeous script as the envelopes I retrieved at the front door with the flowers. The notes I still have yet to read. I open note card #1 and it reads, *"Go to the patio."* Then I open the notecard with the red rose and read, *"Walk over to the table."* The script is so beautifully written.

I walk slowly to the small table, still scanning the patio for any clue as to what is happening. Trying to adjust my eyes to see if someone is there, I see no one. Centered on the table are white tulips and pink roses in a beautiful crystal vase.

Another folded notecard sits atop a nice pile of red and pink rose petals. Again, my name beautifully scripted on the front. I open it slowly and read the typed message, *"Underneath these petals is an amazing surprise ... but only if you're ready for such a treat."*

Now, I like surprises just as much as the next person, but this is on another level. My mind quickly recalls some of the scary movies I used to enjoy. Someone is gonna kill me any moment now and I don't see it coming because I am so enamored by the beauty before me. This scene is a distraction so I am not on guard and ready for the killer. *C'mon Tabitha, that's a bit much,* I think.

I chuckle to myself and scan the patio and nearby area again. *Someone has to be here*, but I don't see a soul. I move what appeared to be the petals of at least a dozen roses. Underneath the beautiful pile was a blue leather box. I gasp and scan the area again. Still no one that I can see. The melodic music changes to "All of Me" by John Legend. Again seemingly on cue. I am being watched. The blue box is sitting atop yet another notecard that read, *"Marry Me."*

I am in complete amazement, again scanning the patio area for at least a glimpse of someone else. I open the little blue box and see the perfect vintage style ring. The center emerald cut diamond has to be at least a carat and a half. The beautiful stone is flanked by a half carat of baguette diamonds in a pavé setting. My mouth drops and I scan the area once more for anyone, at this point, who can tell me what is happening. I have so many questions. Notecard #2 is still in my hand, unread. I take a seat at the table to read the contents:

Tabitha:

You have truly been the light of my life. You came in the most unexpected of ways and what I now see as the perfect time. I am madly in love with you, not the idea of you, but your true self. You see the true me and have a way of making me so comfortable with walking fully in that truth. You bring out the best in me. With you I realize that I never really knew true happiness and contentment. With each passing day, I love you more than the day before. That is why I need you to be the light of my life for the rest of my days. I promise to do everything in my power to show you how much you mean to me for as long as I live. I just need you to say yes!

- I love you,

Just as I finish reading the note, I see this beautiful man lower to one knee and verbally ask me to be his wife.

I say, "Yes!"

About the Author

Talia J. McCoy is a native of Little Rock, AR. She is a multifaceted creative writer who enjoys curating reality based works to connect with her audience. In her debut novel, *Love Lessons*, she does just that.

As a Licensed Clinical Social Worker, Talia beautifully blends social and mental health matters into her works. As an advocate for normalizing help seeking behaviors among the BIPOC community, she weaves relatable stories to include such behaviors.

Read more at https://talaspeaks.com.